HIS CURVY OUTCAST

A SMALL TOWN CURVY GIRL ROMANCE

BOOK BOYFRIENDS WANTED
BOOK SIX

MARY E THOMPSON

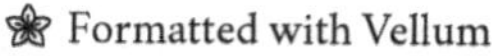 Formatted with Vellum

BOOK BOYFRIENDS WANTED

Welcome! It's great to have you visit MacKellar Cove again. A lot is always going on, but don't worry, we'll catch you up if you've missed anything. Make sure you stay connected and sign up for Mary's newsletter today.

Romancing the Curves comes with subscriber exclusive freebies, sneak peeks, and a first look at everything Mary has to offer. Be the first to know about new releases and sales and all the curves ahead!

SUBSCRIBE NOW AT MARYETHOMPSON.COM

Happy reading!

To anyone who has ever felt like they don't belong...

WILLOW

"No. No, no, no, no, no. You can't do this!" I shouted as I raced to my car.

The cop turned and looked at me, then slid the ticket under my wiper. The bastard.

"I was only in there for a minute. Seriously. It was barely long enough for you to give me a ticket. Can't you just tear that up or something?"

He shook his head, and I tried not to notice how his hair flopped over his forehead in that adorable puppy way. Maybe I should get a dog since I no longer had any friends.

"I'm sorry, but I can't tear it up. And we both know you weren't in there for a minute." He raised an eyebrow and dared me to argue.

Fine, I wasn't, but I wasn't about to admit that to him. I was good at making enemies, and if he wanted to be one, I'd happily take another. It seemed the only way anyone talked to me anymore was to tell me what a disappointment I was.

I glared at him for a long moment, and finally sighed and rolled my eyes. I didn't have time for it. I was busy, too busy for a newbie cop who thought he could do anything in my town.

Yeah, I knew who he was, and I wasn't impressed.

He turned on his heel and started to walk away, then stopped. "You should really watch where you park."

I flipped him off and snatched the ticket from under my wiper. I looked at it and rolled my eyes again. He cited me for blocking a delivery zone. It didn't matter that deliveries didn't happen at that time. Like everything else in my life, I was wrong just for existing.

I got in my car and set my coffee in the cup holder. I would have rather not spent my morning getting coffee from one of my sister's new best friends and getting a ticket from the cop from hell, but I was in a hurry and didn't have time to take care of everything myself. I had an important meeting to get to. And I could not be late.

I sipped the coffee as I pulled out of the parking space I'd made for myself. As soon as I was gone, the delivery truck pulled in to make the daily delivery to Cracked, the best restaurant in town. I hadn't been to Cracked in a long time because of my sister, but I broke down and decided to give myself a little extra luck for today. It was going to be a good day.

Stupid ticket and all.

The drive south was peaceful and quiet. A few cars were on the road, but living in a small town in an area of all small towns meant that there were never many people on the road. I followed the windy path as the sun lifted into the sky and reassured me it was going to be a great day. The kind of day that was made for a fresh start. A new beginning. A new job and a new place to live where no one knew me as Melody's backstabbing little sister.

I could just be Willow Ferguson, a girl from MacKellar

Cove who needed a change. No one needed to know anything else.

I finished my coffee and turned up the radio so I could sing along with the music. The sunshine glittered off the St. Lawrence River to my right. If it weren't freezing outside, I'd definitely have the windows down, but January in upstate New York meant heavy winter coats and defrost blasting the windshield so I could see.

Once I made it to the building where my interview was, I smoothed a hand down my pants and over my brown hair and gave myself another pep talk. After a year of getting berated for everything I did, I needed a pep talk, even if it was only from myself.

"You are awesome," I whispered into my scarf. "You are strong and smart and you can do anything. No one can tell you what you can't do."

I felt better by the time I reached the door and smiled brightly as I walked inside the studio. It was quiet and peaceful, the tans and grays making the small space feel calming. I'd always wanted to teach yoga, but I never let myself dream about it as a career. Too many times I let what others thought get in the way of that, but that was one good thing about not speaking to my sister or caring what she or anyone else thought of me. I was free to do the things I always wanted to do.

"Welcome to Islands Wellness," a woman at the desk said. "Are you here for our next class? It starts in about twenty minutes."

I shook my head and smiled at her. She was cute in a way I'd never been. She was the kind of woman who looked like a yoga instructor. Petite and thin. I started yoga with the hope it would make me look like her, but all it had done was tone my muscles and accentuate my generous curves.

"Actually, I'm here for an interview. Is Kathy available?"

The woman grinned broadly even as her gaze flickered down my curvy figure. "I'm so sorry, of course. She told me you would be coming in, but I didn't think...Let me call her."

"Thank you," I said, taking a step back to look around while the woman made her call. There was a studio visible through the glass to the right, and another one to the left. Behind the desk appeared to be offices and a third studio that was smaller and had blinds on the windows.

The entire space made me feel like I was meant to be there, like it was made for me. Just over an hour from home, getting a job there would mean moving, and moving would mean getting that fresh start I'd been looking for.

I was staring into the first studio, imagining a class in progress, when a voice behind me made every hair on my body stand up.

"Willow Ferguson. I wondered if that was really you. I never in a million years thought you would be coming to me for something."

I turned and nearly ran out the door. Kathy Rogers was standing in front of me looking perfect in her pink tank top and black leggings. She had a perfect figure and perfect hair and perfect everything, right down to a massive perfect ring on her left hand.

"Kathy Rogers? I didn't realize you were...I thought I was supposed to meet a Kathy Davis."

She walked right over to me and hugged me, her perfect fake smile in place the entire time. "I got married right out of college. My husband is crazy rich and bought me this studio a few years ago. He knew I wanted to help people learn to be healthy." Her gaze slid down my oversized body. Her perfect smile faltered at my not-perfect chubby waist and thick thighs.

I was toned, but I wasn't thin. My mom always said I was big-boned, which I took to mean I was fat. Maybe that wasn't fair, but standing next to the woman who made high school a living hell for me, I felt like I was the failed joke of a star on one of those weight loss shows on TV.

"Anyway, when I saw your name on the resume, I just had to have you come down so we could catch up," Kathy said.

I forced a smile and saw my dreams of working there vanish before my eyes. I wanted nothing more than to tell her to go to hell and walk out the door, but I was trying to be a better person.

It sucked.

I followed Kathy to her office and took a seat opposite her glass desk. The placard on the edge read *Kathy Davis, owner*. Her walls were a soft green color with serene pictures artfully displayed. Everything in her office screamed money and class, two words I never would have used to describe her when we were growing up.

"So, your resume says you don't have any experience teaching yoga. Is that the case?"

All of my perfectly reasonable explanations went out the window. All my rehearsed answers sounded flat and dumb sitting there. The only thing I wanted to do was cry because I had so many dreams that hinged on me getting this job. But I knew it wasn't going to happen. There was no way.

I went through the interview and tried to make myself sound like I was worth a gamble, but every question out of Kathy's mouth said she just brought me there for a laugh. She never had any intention of giving me a shot.

And why would she? I had no training or experience. I had no plans for how I would do it. I was winging it, like I'd done everything else in my life, something my mother reminded me of constantly.

I was no Melody. I wasn't the one with the husband and the kid and the organized life. I was the screw up. The one who'd almost ruined my sister's life because I wanted what she had.

I walked out of the interview numb. When Kathy said she'd let me know soon, I couldn't handle anymore. I turned on her and said, "You know what, don't bother. We both know you aren't going to hire me. You only brought me down here to show me how much better your life is than mine. You win. I give up. I'm not interested in the job anymore. I don't want it."

She scoffed and crossed her arms. A smirk curled her lips. "You aren't qualified. You have no training. You've never taught a class. Why would I hire you, even if I wanted to? You're the same person you were in high school. You think you can do whatever you want, but we're adults. I have responsibilities to my clients. They're not going to come here to take yoga from..." Her scornful gaze slid down my body and I felt like I weighed a thousand pounds. "...you. They want to be healthy and fit. This isn't a joke for them, or for me. But thanks for coming in."

I sucked back the emotion in my throat and swallowed roughly. I didn't bother to say anything else. I wanted to cry, to tell her how horrible she was, to get revenge on her. But she was right. No one would want to take yoga from me. No one would want to hire me. I was working the same job I had in high school. I was still the same person. I hadn't changed a bit.

And I had no one to blame but myself.

I WAS STILL SULKING the next day when I got off work. My shift at Kerri's Boutique was a long one, and I was tired. I needed a drink, and even though I was sure I would regret it, when my coworkers invited me out with them, I said yes.

"Seriously?" Brittany asked me. She and I had been casual friends for years. We had gone out more than a few times to pick up guys and get crazy, but since my fallout with Melody, I hadn't gone out at all.

I shrugged. "I need to stop hiding. Especially since it appears as though I'm going to die in this town."

"You didn't get the job?" she asked.

I shook my head. Brittany was the only person who knew I had an interview. I didn't tell her when it was, but she knew it was soon.

"We need drinks. Lots of them. Because I'm happy you're staying, and you should be, too. There are plenty of hot men here, and there's no reason to be upset when we live in a beautiful place."

I laughed with Brittany and tried to feel some of her excitement. I loved my hometown, but I hadn't felt like it was really home since Melody and I stopped talking. Maybe getting back to the things I did before would help. Especially since I wasn't going anywhere. The job with Kathy was the only potential one I had, and that wasn't happening.

Brittany got us drinks while I found a table at O'Kelley's, the local hang out. I looked around the bar while I walked, checking to make sure none of Melody or Ramsey's friends were there. I wasn't interested in running into anyone who would report back to my sister or brother-in-law that I was there or what I was doing.

"There is a hottie at the bar," Brittany said as she delivered our drinks. "I'm going to see if he wants to dance. Have you spotted anyone yet?"

I shook my head and picked up my drink. Brittany went in search of her hottie and left me at the table. I sipped my drink and tried not to feel out of place. Had everyone gotten younger since I was there last? Jeez, I felt old even though I was only thirty-one. The people who looked older than me were in pairs and groups. The only single people there looked far younger. When had that happened?

Brittany didn't come back to the table and after dirty looks from groups who couldn't find a table of their own, I decided it was about time to call it a night.

I found an unoccupied bar stool and waited for a bartender to come over so I could settle our tab. If Brittany was still there, she could open a new one, but I didn't want to risk running out on our drinks.

I groaned when I finally got the attention of the owner, Hudson Grant. He was one of Ramsey's closest friends, which meant he was not a fan of mine at all. I'd hoped one of the other bartenders would help me, but of course my luck was shit.

Hudson walked over and set a fresh drink in front of me. I sipped the nearly empty one I had and narrowed my eyes at him. He wasn't my friend, so there had to be a catch. "What's this for?"

"A peace offering," Hudson said.

"From you?" I raised one eyebrow in question.

Hudson snorted. "No. From him." He nodded toward the end of the bar.

I followed his nod and froze. "No. I don't want it. Not from him."

Hudson shrugged. "Then don't drink it. I don't care."

Hudson walked away and left me staring at the offending drink. I glared at the cop who wrote me a ticket the day before. Did he really think a drink would make up for it?

I shook my head and pushed the drink away. I was not going to drink it.

"Did I guess wrong?" a voice next to me asked. He sat on the stool to my right and acted like he belonged there.

"What do you want?"

He shrugged. "Just trying to be nice. You looked like you could use a drink. Another one."

"Not from you," I said firmly.

"Well, I guess I thought wrong. Have a good night."

He walked away, disappearing into the crowd. I stared at the drink again, debating. I didn't want it from him, but I definitely wanted it.

I glanced around, but he was nowhere to be seen. I brought the drink closer. He didn't have to know. I lifted it and smelled the glass. Vodka. I smiled. Another glance around, then I tipped the glass up and drained it. The liquid burned my throat as it slid down. I closed my eyes and relished the feel. It was good. So damn good.

I sucked in a breath and set the glass back down. Then I looked up and saw him across the bar, watching me. He grinned, the ass, and lifted his glass.

Dammit.

ROWAN

I loved the pissed off look on her face. Maybe it was cruel, but it turned me on in ways I shouldn't enjoy so much. Most of the women in the tiny town I'd chosen to hide in were happy to throw themselves at a police officer, but that one…she would have thrown just about anything else at me instead.

But that drink was the key. She was a sucker for vodka, and she couldn't resist it.

The second she walked in, I asked Hudson about her. He was happy enough to warn me off of her, but I wasn't very good at following directions. Especially directions that meant nothing. I was definitely playing with fire with her, but it would be worth it.

She glared at me and slammed the glass down on the bar. I tried not to smirk, but that feistiness was what had been missing from my life for months. I needed it.

I turned my drink up and drained the last of it. When I set it on the bar, I glanced over at her again, but dammit, she was gone. I scanned the bar, but there were too many people for me to see where she was. I stalked through the whole place and finally admitted she left.

Slippery. I shook my head and laughed. She lived up to the reputation Hudson told me about.

I got another drink and nursed it at the bar. A part of me wanted to take one of the many women who flirted with me up on their offer, but I wasn't all that interested in the rest of them. The one I wanted was already gone.

I walked outside to get a minute of fresh air and debated heading home for the night. I was almost ready to when the door opened and she walked out.

She didn't see me at first. She paused on the sidewalk and dug through her purse. I wanted to know what she was looking for. I wanted to know a lot of things about her. In that moment, I wanted to know what she tasted like.

"Leaving already?" I asked, finally letting her know I was there.

She jumped and spun toward me, dropping her purse to the ground. The contents dribbled out onto the snow covered sidewalk and she groaned.

"Just my fucking luck."

"Why don't I help you?" I offered.

"Why don't you go to hell?"

I chuckled and crouched down to retrieve her things. Lipgloss, a crumpled sticky note, and a tampon were closest to me. I held them in my hand for her to take them.

She glared at me and shoved them back into her bag before standing and throwing the bag over her shoulder. "What the hell are you doing out here? Stalking innocent women?"

"We both know there is nothing innocent about you."

She sucked in a breath and lifted her gaze to meet mine. That spark was back, daring me. Demanding I push her just a little farther.

I took a step toward her, and she didn't retreat. She tilted her head back to maintain eye contact with me. And when I got right in her personal space, she raised her hands to my shoulders.

"What are you doing?" she whispered.

"I'm going to kiss you," I said. I didn't give her a chance to argue or tell me she didn't want me to. I knew she did. I could see it in her eyes, and when my lips touched hers, I could feel it in the way she responded to me.

She tried to pull back a second later, but I wasn't letting her go yet. I held her close, and another second later she was melting into me. Her hands slid up my shoulders and around my neck. She tilted her head to the side and teased my lips with her tongue.

I groaned and spun her, walking forward until her back hit the wall of O'Kelley's. She whimpered but didn't stop. Her nails bit into my neck and she sucked hard on my tongue.

My cock liked that.

Someone else walked out of O'Kelley's, letting the noise of the crowd break us apart. The guy looked at us and nodded, then kept walking.

I glared after him then turned back to Willow. She was already closed off. Her gaze was cast down, and she was biting her lip. "That never happened," she said.

"It can keep happening."

She shook her head and pushed at my shoulders. I backed off, reluctantly. "No. It's...no. You gave me a ticket, and you're friends with..."

I raised an eyebrow in question, waiting for her to tell me who I wasn't supposed to be friends with even though I was sure I knew.

She shook her head. "This isn't a good idea."

"Then how about you let me walk you home? Make sure you get home okay?"

She snorted. "Nice try. Nothing exciting happens in MacKellar Cove. I'm not worried."

"But—"

"See you around," she called as she hurried away, leaving me to watch her go with nothing I could do about it.

I HAD ALMOST MADE it to my desk the next morning when my name rang out across the bullpen. I knew better than to think I would get away with talking to her, or kissing her, but I didn't expect it to become public so quickly.

I turned to face Rucker, the officer assigned to show me around when I arrived in town. I couldn't say he was my partner because that was just...but I rode with him when I first started in MacKellar Cove. A part of me wondered if we were becoming friends, but I wasn't sure about that one either. "Yeah?" I asked him.

"What's up with you and the evil seed?"

Rucker didn't pull any punches. He had a tendency to be blunt to the point of pissing people off far too often. And when it came to her, he didn't care.

"Nothing," I said, and kept walking.

"Why'd you buy her a drink?"

"Damn small town," I muttered.

"You knew I'd find out. Hudson is like a schoolgirl with a secret. He can't keep anything to himself. And after what she pulled last year, we're all on high alert with her."

I shrugged and lied my ass off. "I just bought her a drink."

"Yeah, but why?"

"Because she looked like she needed it."

His brows went up. He crossed his arms over his chest. He leaned back and appraised me.

I didn't like being evaluated. I'd been found wanting far too often in my life, and it wasn't a fun situation to be in.

"Do you know her?"

I shook my head. Another lie. I knew better.

"It's probably best if you stay away from her. She's bad news."

I nodded once. "Understood. Although last I checked, I make my own decisions."

Rucker snorted. "Trust me. This is a decision you want to agree with me on. She almost ruined Ramsey's marriage. She tried to break them up by manipulating his wife. All because she had some misguided crush on him. She couldn't see that she was the only one who was feeling something. She thought if she broke up their marriage that she could have Ramsey for herself. Fifteen years of twisting things and trying to end their marriage. You don't want to be involved with someone like that."

I rubbed my jaw and thought about it. Hudson didn't share that much the night before. She definitely sounded a little insane, but how much of it was true. I'd been on the receiving end of one too many lies a time or two, and it wasn't easy to come back from something like that. And that was living in a city when no one really gave a shit.

"Good to know. Thanks," I told Rucker. I continued to my seat and got my day started. It had been a while since I had to run my actions past another person. I wasn't about to start that again.

Not after the way it ended last time.

Life in a small town was different than what I thought it would be. For some reason, I thought I'd be able to be anonymous. I was definitely wrong about that. People I'd never met before knew my name and asked me how my day was. Going to a call was an exercise in patience instead of an opportunity to do my job. And the worst part of all of it was not letting the people get to me. I had no interest in getting attached because I wasn't going to be there much longer. Not that anyone else knew.

I was about to head out on patrol when the captain called me into his office. When he told me to close the door, every fiber of my being said to run, but I took a seat instead.

"I need a favor," Captain Reynolds said. "The local high school needs someone to come down and do a presentation. It's something we do every year for the entire student body. We want them to know they can come to us, but also be afraid of getting in trouble. It takes a little bit of delicate work to strike the right balance."

"And you think I'm the right guy for this?" Captain Reynolds was the only person at the precinct who knew all the details about why I was there. He agreed to the temporary transfer. My former captain was a good friend of his and the two of them said this was for the best for me. I wasn't entirely sure they were right, but I also wasn't given a choice. It was either this or leave the force.

"I do. A lot of our officers have been there over the years. These kids need to see someone new, someone they don't know. Roberts has a kid in the high school. Munez has two. Rucker, Allen, and Dewey were there in the last three years."

"So, I'm the only option?"

Captain Reynolds shook his head. "No, but I think this will be good for you. We also use this as a recruiting opportunity. These kids are all too young to join the force, but it opens up a line of communication to us for the ones who might be interested one day."

"You get a lot?"

Captain Reynolds shook his head. "No, but about every other year we get one or two. The high school is small, and with less than a hundred kids graduating each year, getting one or two in a couple years isn't bad."

"I'm not sure I'm the right one for this."

Captain Reynolds shrugged. "I disagree. I think you're exactly right for this. And you're going to do it."

I wanted to argue, but I followed orders when they mattered. I didn't push back against authority. I knew if rules weren't followed, bad things happened. I'd seen it happen with my own eyes. Ignoring the advice of friends was one thing. Ignoring the order of my boss was another entirely.

"Yes, sir."

Captain Reynolds nodded once. "The program is Friday. You have a meeting today at one with the principal of the school to go over everything. All the details are in your inbox."

"Yes, sir," I said again.

He held my gaze a minute longer then nodded for me to leave.

I went back to my desk and read through the information sent to me. It sounded reasonable enough, but I still didn't like the idea.

I worked on figuring out how I could get out of the assignment right up until the time I walked into the high school. It was a tiny building, only one floor with a center hall and two wings. The guard at the door took my name and had me wait until someone came to get me before he let me through the security door.

"Thank you so much for coming today," the woman said when she shook my hand. "Captain Reynolds said you would be perfect for this. We always appreciate having someone come talk to our students."

"Of course," I said, not really feeling the warm fuzzy that she was. "Can I ask who you are?"

"Oh, I'm sorry. I forget you don't know me. I'm Robin Thomas. I'm the principal here. I've been in this job for eight years now. I grew up in MacKellar Cove and taught here for sixteen years, then I decided to move up the ranks when the principal I taught under put in for retirement. There aren't a lot of opportunities in a school like this, but I didn't mind because I love teaching. There's a part of me that still misses working with the kids every day, you know?"

I smiled and nodded because I had no idea what she was talking about or why she was telling me so much. It was the curse of a small town. Everyone knew everyone else's business and they expected it, so if you didn't know something, they shared. Way too much.

"How about you? Why did you become a police officer?" she asked as we pushed into the auditorium.

"I never liked art," I said.

Mrs. Thomas laughed like she thought it was a joke but her laughter died when she saw my face. "Oh, um, that makes sense?"

I didn't elaborate like she obviously wanted me to. She didn't really want to hear about my past. She just wanted something she could share with others. Everyone wanted gossip, and they were all looking for whatever gossip they could find on me.

She forced a smile after a minute and turned to the small auditorium. "Okay, well, this is where we'll have you on Friday. We bring in the students by grade level, so it'll be four presentations. We have a projector for you if you have a slideshow. We also have a mic and will have teachers here to help you get everything set up."

"Sounds good," I said, unsure why I was really there if she was just telling me about the auditorium.

"The topic for this year is Spotting Spirals, so, of course, your talk will have to be about that. How to recognize when a friend or relative is going in a bad direction, what to do about it, and getting help if something is bigger than you can handle. We also have a psychologist coming in to talk, but usually the police officers are better able to connect with the kids."

It all made sense. Captain Reynolds set me up. He knew exactly what he was asking me to do, and he set me up.

My entire body broke out in a cold sweat as I pictured Sanders' face.

"We have a pretty good student body, but because they've all known each other forever, it's hard to stand up to each other sometimes. Even the kids who don't run in the same circles grew up together and know each other. They need some reminders that it's okay to ask for help. That it isn't a betrayal to go to a teacher or a counselor if they think someone is in over their head. As adults, we know this, but these kids aren't always willing to reach out."

"I got it," I snapped at her.

She narrowed her eyes and tilted her head to the side. Her short gray-blonde hair shifted with the move as her hazel eyes appraised me. "Is there something I need to know, Officer?"

"No," I said sharply. "I understand the assignment."

"And it's one you're capable of handling? Because these students need to know you're someone they can speak to. We tell them if they can't go to a parent or a teacher, to find someone else they trust. A coach, an officer, or someone else they feel comfortable talking to. If you aren't able to show these students that they can speak to you, this isn't going to be a good thing."

"I got it," I said again. My patience was slipping, but that was the least of my concern. Patience was one thing, but my ability to keep my lunch down was another. My body felt like every nerve was exposed, like even the brush of the heat forced into the room from the high up vents was scalding me. I needed to get the hell out of there.

"Officer Masterson—"

"I need to go, Mrs. Thomas. Thank you for showing me around. I will be here Friday."

I turned and walked to the auditorium door, not waiting for her to follow me or escort me from the building. I couldn't be in there another minute. I needed fresh air and clarity. Clarity that would only come with putting my fist through something.

Instead of going back to the precinct, I went straight home. The punching bag in my spare bedroom was calling to me.

I stripped my shirt off as I walked inside. I locked up my gun, then went to the spare room. The first hit stung my hand since I didn't bother with gloves. The second pissed me off. The third brought a flash of pain with it. The fourth made me feel sick. After that, I pushed everything out and beat on the bag until my knuckles were raw. I screamed out the last of my pain and kicked the bag.

I had no idea how I was going to talk to a bunch of teenagers about recognizing when someone was in a bad spot. It sounded easy enough on the outside, but I was supposed to be there as an authority, as someone who had advice and knew what to say. But it was all lies. I had no idea what to tell them. And if I said anything, it wouldn't fix anything and it wouldn't change anything.

Because at the end of the day, I still failed to see the signs. I still failed to recognize the issue. And I still failed to report it in time.

At the end of the day, my partner was in a spiral that I never saw coming, and he killed himself because he couldn't see any other way out.

And every day I had to live with the guilt of knowing I could have saved him and I didn't.

WILLOW

"Ooh, he's yummy," Brittany said with a salacious grin. "That's a definite yes."

We were at work and folding shirts. At least, I was folding shirts. She was staring at her phone. "What are you doing?"

"Setting up a hookup for tonight. Give me your phone. I'll get you someone."

"What are you talking about?"

"The dating app. Book Boyfriends Wanted. Everyone around here uses it. Don't tell me you aren't on it."

I shook my head and kept working. Online dating was not for me. I'd heard too many horror stories. Besides, that app was designed by Melody's friend, Karissa, so that was a big hell, no.

"I'll create an account for you. No wonder you're so miserable. You need to knock out the cobwebs in there and have a little fun."

"I don't have cobwebs in there," I argued.

"When's the last time you had sex?"

I opened my mouth and realized I had no idea. Before I

could recover, Brittany snatched my phone out of my apron pocket. "Hey!"

"It's for your own good," she said, turning away from me as a customer walked up.

"Do you have these in purple?" the woman asked, holding up a pair of heels.

I forced a smile in her direction while I tried to see if Brittany was indeed creating an account for me. The grin on her face said she was. Last time I tell her my passcode.

"We do. I'll show you."

I answered a few questions for the customer and showed her a necklace that would work well with the shoes. I'd been waiting to buy both for months, so I had an idea of how to make them look even better. The only problem for me was where in the world I would wear them. Heels didn't do well in an old town with uneven sidewalks. And impressing a guy was impossible when he'd pulled your pigtails in elementary school or dated your friends in high school.

I needed a new town. Then I could wear the shoes and the necklace and do whatever the hell I wanted.

"All set," Brittany said when I rejoined her. She handed my phone back to me. "You are meeting JustVisiting for drinks at eight tonight at O'Kelley's. You're welcome."

"Tell me you're joking," I said.

Brittany shook her head and grinned. "Nope. He's sarcastic and grumpy, like you. The two of you will be a perfect match."

I rolled my eyes and shoved my phone back in my pocket with the mental note to change my code.

"You have to wear something red. You look amazing in red, and I told him to look for you in jeans, since you always wear jeans, and a red top."

"So, if I don't want to meet this guy, I can wear something else?"

"Nope, because I have his screen name and can message him, too."

"You're not my friend."

She raised a dark eyebrow. "I'm your only friend."

The truth hit me hard. She was right. Brittany was the only person who didn't turn away from me when Melody and I stopped speaking. Not that I had a ton of people I was close to, but everyone took her side. Except Brittany.

"You're right. Thank you."

The rest of our shift went by quickly and before I knew it, I was in my red top and jeans walking into O'Kelley's for the second time in less than a week. And going there to meet a guy. What the hell was I thinking?

Brittany got us drinks again, and I found a table. It was quieter than it had been Tuesday, and not as many people were hovering around tables. When Brittany came back, she sipped her drink and looked around.

"I don't think either of our matches are here yet, but there are plenty of good looking guys around."

I looked with her and found myself unable to get excited about any of them. A year ago, I could go out with Melody and not think twice about going home with someone, but now…I was pretty sure she broke me.

"Did your guy message you?" Brittany asked.

I pulled out my phone and opened the app. I still couldn't believe she created an account for me. "How do I use this?"

"Go to the envelope for messages. Your matches are under the heart. Profile stuff is at the gear. It's pretty simple, which is totally genius."

I clicked on the envelope and saw messages from a few different people. "There's a ton in here."

Brittany grabbed my phone. "Those are all your matches who've reached out. Nice."

"Seriously?" I asked. It was nice to feel like someone wanted me, even if they didn't really know who I was.

"Yep. Ooh, my guy just got here. I'm going to go find him. Have fun tonight!"

I waved as Brittany walked off. I sipped my beer and tried to pretend I wasn't wishing I had a vodka tonic at home.

"Here you go," Piper, one of the servers, said. She set two drinks down on the table.

"What are these for?"

"I was told to say your match is here and he's going to join you in a minute," Piper said with a grin.

"Seriously? He's here? Oh, God, I'm going to be sick."

"Why?" Piper asked, her grin sliding off her face.

"Is he cute? Do you know him? You know everyone. Am I going to be disappointed?"

Piper shook her head and grinned again. "You're not going to be disappointed. He's totally cute, and yes, I know him. You have nothing to worry about."

I sucked in a deep breath and nodded. "Thank you. Sorry. I know you're not supposed to talk to me."

"Why not?"

"Because I'm Melody's sister and you're all friends or whatever."

Piper chuckled. "I like Melody, but I'm not going to choose sides on something between sisters. That wouldn't be fair."

I eyed her closely and saw nothing but kindness. That was definitely a shock, and something that calmed me more than I cared to admit. "Thank you, Piper."

Piper nodded and put her hand on mine. "Of course. Have fun, Willow."

I nodded and picked up the drink in front of me. I brought it to my lips and was surprised when it was a vodka tonic. How did he know? Brittany had to have put something in my profile.

I closed my eyes and enjoyed the subtle burn and the fizz as the drink worked its way into my system. I was vaguely aware of someone joining me but kept my eyes closed to take him in for just a moment longer.

He smelled amazing, like he'd just showered with something that was designed to make men into sex gods. His presence comforted me in a weird way, like I could feel him and felt safe with him around. His knee brushed mine under the table, and the warmth of him sent a spark through all of me.

Then he opened his mouth. "I didn't see this coming."

I groaned. "Seriously?" I asked as I lifted my lids, disappointment forcing the desire and hope to the edges of my body. It was still there, tingling in my fingertips and telling me to ignore anything that kept us apart, but I couldn't ignore it.

"I shouldn't be surprised, but you don't seem like the type to join an online dating thing," Rowan said with a smirk.

"Apparently you are, so why shouldn't I be?"

He shrugged. "I don't know anyone here. You know everyone. I figured it was easier to meet someone when you know everyone."

"Not even a little. I could tell you a story about just about everyone here. I know details of their lives that I wouldn't know if we hadn't grown up in the same town. It sucks."

"Is that why you agreed to meet me? Because you didn't think we knew each other?"

"No. I didn't really agree to this at all. My friend set up my account. She did all this today while I was working."

"Ah, I see," Rowan said. He leaned back in his seat and picked up the glass in front of him. He stretched out his legs and brushed his calves against mine.

I couldn't deny that there was a spark there. As much as I didn't want to find him attractive, he was. His dark hair that slid over his forehead at times, those eyes that seemed to be able to peer into my soul, and those hands…the thought of them on my body again made every cell vibrate in anticipation.

But I couldn't sleep with him. I couldn't do anything with him. Kissing him was bad enough, anything else would be a disaster. Not only was he a new friend of Ramsey's, he was the asshole who wrote me a ticket. I'd never gotten a ticket for parking illegally before he came to town.

"Is that your way of saying you aren't interested?" Rowan asked.

It took me a second to remember what we were talking about. He was giving me an out. A way to turn him down. But in reality, it was a way for him to get out of this without looking like the asshole. He could say he didn't know it was me, and that nothing happened.

I glanced around the bar and saw Hudson watching us. He did not look happy about it. I was the town pariah, and the newbie was talking to me, trapped. It didn't matter that I didn't know who he was, if I didn't let him off the hook, things would only get worse for me.

"Yeah, I'm not interested," I forced out. I lifted my drink and took another sip to keep anything else inside.

"That's not the way it seemed the other day. When you kissed me back."

"I told you that was a mistake. That can't happen again. And neither can this. Whatever this is."

Rowan held my gaze for another long moment then nodded and grabbed his drink. He got up from the chair and walked to the bar.

Hudson was in front of him the moment he sat down, and

I forced myself to look away. There was no reason to wonder. I didn't like him anyway.

Piper came back a few minutes later and asked what happened. Another spy. Another person looking for something to tell my sister so she could hate me even more. I told Piper we weren't a good match and went to the bathroom.

I had every intention of leaving when I got back to the table, but Brittany was sitting there looking annoyed. "What's wrong?" I asked her.

"My guy was a total dick. He wasn't even worth sleeping with. Where's your guy?"

"Didn't work out," I told her.

"Why not? I thought he was good."

I shrugged. "No worries."

"Then we need to dance. We need to find guys tonight who are live and in person and have some fun. Come on."

I let Brittany pull me toward the dance floor. I told myself she was right, and I let the music pull me in. Dancing felt good. It released all the tension I'd been carrying around, and it let me move my body. She was right. I definitely needed it.

A guy came up behind Brittany and danced with her. She turned toward him and wrapped her arms around his neck. Another guy danced with me, running his hands up and down my sides.

I tried to enjoy it, but I found myself wishing I was anywhere but there.

The song changed and the guy behind me went to find someone else to dance with. Brittany was making out with her guy in the corner. I danced alone for a few minutes, trying to convince myself I was having fun, but I was just ready to get out of there.

I caught Brittany's attention and told her I was going to leave. She waved me off and went right back to the guy she was with. I almost missed feeling like that. Being able to let my guard down and not worry about who the guy was or what he thought of me.

Or what I thought of myself.

I headed back toward our table so I could grab my jacket. People moved all around me, forcing me to walk around the group of people dancing instead of going straight through toward our table.

I made it into the open and nearly came face-to-face with Melody and Ramsey. I froze for half a second then turned quickly before they spotted me and disappeared back into the crowd.

What were they doing there? They never went out during the week. And they never had anyone to stay with Amber. A lot had changed in the last year. I had to admit I didn't know what was going on in their lives.

All night, I tried to convince myself that I belonged there, that staying in MacKellar Cove was a good idea, but one glance at my sister and I knew I was wrong. MacKellar Cove was no longer my home, and pretending it was was a mistake.

I worked through the dancing crowd again, fighting my way to the table. Instead of grabbing my coat and getting the hell out of there, I sat down and stared at them. I couldn't move. It hurt too much to see them and be on the outside.

Growing up, I could say anything to my sister. I shared every part of myself with her. We were best friends, and she never once turned her back on me. I didn't turn on her either. I worshipped her. She amazed me every day. She made everything seem effortless, especially falling in love.

Ramsey was the first boy who paid me any attention. It didn't matter that he was there to see Melody, he always said hi to me and asked how I was doing. He made me feel special, even though I was barely a teenager.

It hurt to think about them. To know a year ago, I was

spending time with Melody and my niece, Amber. I was in their lives. And with one admission, all that changed. My sister forgave Ramsey and took him back like nothing had happened, but I was the outcast. The one no one in town wanted anything to do with. I was on the outside looking in.

Piper was at the table next to me and I waved her over when she was done with them. "Can I get you something else?" she asked with a smile.

"Another vodka tonic, please."

"Got it. I'll be right back."

I thanked her and spun the straw in the watered down drink on the table. I should have just left, but I was a glutton for punishment apparently.

Piper returned with my drink and I thanked her again. I was trying to be nice. I didn't think it would do any good, but I was trying.

I glanced over to where Melody and Ramsey sat, holding hands and looking like they couldn't get enough of each other. I didn't want to look. I wasn't a part of their world anymore. But I couldn't help but wish I was.

"Someone you know?" Rowan asked, sitting down opposite me.

I shook my head. "Used to." I still hadn't figured him out. I pushed him away, but he kept coming back. No matter how many times I told him we weren't a good idea, he was there. He clearly had options since half the town seemed to flirt with him, but he kept coming back to me. A part of me liked that I wasn't alone, but another part wondered why he was bothering with me.

"Him or her?"

I drew a breath and turned my focus to Rowan instead of my sister and brother-in-law. It was no longer my concern who was watching my niece or if they were happy. It was time to find my own happiness. Even if it was temporary.

"Want to get out of here?"

He raised a dark eyebrow and held my gaze for a long moment. I was sure he'd say no, but he drained his fresh drink and nodded. Just once, like he was sure.

Glad one of us was.

4

The sharp bite of cold against my face was a welcome relief after the warmth of the bar. Having Rowan walk me home…the jury was still out on that one.

"Are you okay?" Rowan asked as we turned north.

I nodded and buried my chin in my scarf. "Great."

He snorted like he knew the single word was sarcasm. Maybe he did. "You were on your own tonight?"

I shook my head. "No. My friend was there. She set up a date with someone from the app, too."

"The friend who completed your profile?"

"Yeah. She said I need to get out there more."

"Bad breakup?" he asked.

I breathed a mirthless laugh. "Something like that."

"What's the worst excuse you've ever heard for ending a relationship?" He shoved his hands in his pockets and looked at me expectantly. He raised one dark eyebrow and speared me with those dark eyes again. I couldn't understand how he could see right into me, but I felt it.

Or maybe he just knew more about me than he was

letting on. Plenty of people in town were likely more than happy to tell him I wasn't worth the trouble.

"Worst excuse?" I asked.

He nodded. "Yep. I heard a guy tell his girlfriend they couldn't keep seeing each other because he hated the color of her hair."

"What? Did she dye it?"

He shook his head. "Nope. He just woke up one day and decided he didn't like it. Ended things."

"Was that guy you?"

He barked a laugh and shook his head. "No. An old friend."

"That's cryptic."

He didn't say anything else, just kept walking.

"Okay, fine, the worst excuse I ever heard was that she thought he would be different. And this was after almost six months of dating."

"Thought he would be different. What does that even mean?"

"It means she expected him to be better in bed."

"Really?"

I shrugged. "Definitely."

"Was that you?" he asked with a laugh.

"Unfortunately, yes."

"He sucked in bed?"

"Unfortunately, yes."

Rowan chuckled. "No one should have to suffer through mediocre sex. Why even bother if it doesn't blow your mind?"

"That's what I keep saying. It's why I haven't...Anyway, I agree."

"Why you haven't what?" he pressed.

"Nothing. Don't worry about it."

He pulled me to a stop in the middle of the sidewalk and

turned me to face him. His eyes were deadly serious. His shoulders were pulled up to his ears, his feet tapping on the sidewalk. "Why you haven't what?"

I took a deep breath and found myself unable to lie to him. I did not like that feeling. "Had sex in a while."

"You? I guess you have good locks on your door."

"Huh?"

"You had to be fighting them off."

I snorted. "Hardly. Most of the guys in town grew up with either me or my sister or are friends with my brother-in-law. I'm not new to anyone."

"You're new to me," he said firmly.

My breath hitched. I glanced up at him. He was staring right back, the heat in his eyes chasing away the cold night air.

He stepped closer to me and I forgot how to breathe entirely. His cold hand cupped my jaw and tilted my head up. His eyes held mine, and I leaned toward him. He drew me in slowly, our bodies growing closer together until our lips touched.

We both froze for an instant, like the kiss was a surprise. Then he took a step closer and slid his hand to my throat. He pressed his thumb under my jaw and tilted my head back farther, then licked his way into my mouth.

I moaned softly as his tongue brushed against mine. His other hand reached behind me and brought our bodies closer together. My hands went to his chest, trapped between us but needing to touch him. The thickness of our coats dulled any sensations beyond the kiss, but I didn't care.

His tongue swept through my mouth and learned every inch. He tangled with my tongue, teasing me before pressing thickly inside. I groaned, wanting more, and he pulled back.

Before I could protest, he grabbed my hand and dragged me down the darkened street. I didn't ask how he knew which house was mine or how he knew I rented a room above the garage. I just accepted it and unlocked the door.

Inside, he pulled me back in, his hands and mouth learning everything there was to know about me. I nipped at his lip and earned a growl. He pressed my back to the front door and ensured I didn't move with a thick thigh between my legs.

"What do you want, Willow?"

"Excuse me?"

"What do you want? From me. Right now. Do you want me to go or stay? Do you want me to kiss you or more? What do you want?"

"I want you to take off your clothes." I'd never been shy during sex. Or really, any other time. I knew I had to take what I wanted from life or I'd never get anything. My parents weren't warm and fuzzy people, and they never spoiled us, so I learned early I had to grab what I wanted and claim it as my own.

A lot of people said I was a bitch for that, but they were just jealous that they didn't have the same attitude. I never understood waiting around for something to happen. I made things happen.

And with Rowan, I was going to make this happen. I didn't plan it. Hell, until he kissed me, I wasn't even sure I wanted it. But I was going to get it.

He stepped back and dropped his leather jacket to the floor. He toed off his boots as he unbuttoned his jeans. He reached back and tugged his shirt off with one hand. Then his hands went to his jeans and his eyes lifted to mine.

"Am I the only one taking off my clothes?"

I raised an eyebrow at him and grinned. He watched me strip to my bra and panties, both boring teal cotton.

"Don't stop there."

"Bedroom," I told him, nodding toward the only door in the tiny apartment.

Rowan reached for me and brought our bodies together. He brushed the hair from my neck and licked his way from my collarbone up to my ear. He nibbled on my earlobe and across my jaw. When our lips met, he didn't waste any time thrusting his tongue between my lips.

The entire time, his hands roamed my body, lighting me up. He guided me backward until we made it into my room. He pulled back long enough to see where the bed was. His large hands cupped my ass and lifted me effortlessly.

"You're going to hurt yourself," I argued, trying to squirm out of his grasp.

"Not if you stop moving. Damn, woman."

I stopped fighting him and tried not to worry about him dropping me. A size twenty ass was not usually carried around. I never had been before, and I definitely didn't expect it from him.

"You're beautiful," he said, nipping the exposed skin of my breast. "Stunning."

I drew in a breath and tried to believe his words, but I knew they were just to butter me up. He didn't realize I was going to sleep with him whether he complimented me or not. I wasn't doing it for the ego boost. It was all about sex for me.

He lowered me to the mattress gently and scanned my face and body with his eyes. I wanted to cover up, or kick him out, but I didn't do either. If he found me wanting, or if this was all a big joke to him, I wasn't going to back down. I was stronger than him.

Then he licked his lips and pressed his cock against my core. The barrier of my panties and his jeans stopped his progress, but there was no mistaking that he wanted me as much as I wanted him.

"Condom," he breathed. He reached into his pocket and grabbed one, holding it in his teeth while he shoved his jeans and boxer briefs to the floor. He kicked out of them and tore the foil wrapper while I removed my panties and admired his body.

He was blanketed with muscles. His arms bulged and his abs danced. His cock was thick and surrounded by a neat nest of trimmed dark hair. His thighs were strong, and those hands…they pressed my thighs wide and teased my entrance. One finger slid into me. He groaned with me as he withdrew, coating my skin as he teased his way to my clit.

He held my gaze with his as his fingers manipulated me. I bit my lip and tried to hold back, wanting the orgasm to last. I was on the edge, ready to fall over, but I wasn't ready. I needed more.

I'd missed the connection sex brought with another person. I missed knowing that we were in it together. For years, sex was just fun, but somewhere along the line, sex became more. Even with strangers, sex was about making sure someone else was happy.

Everyone in my life thought I was selfish, but not during sex. During sex, I wanted to see the man I was with lose his mind. I wanted to watch him go crazy and know I gave him that.

Rowan's eyes fell to half-mast and he swallowed roughly. His fingers stroked over my clit, pinching and pulling at the throbbing nub until I was unable to hold back.

"Oh," I moaned. "Yes."

At the first sign that I was going over, Rowan thrust hard into me and shattered that last little bit holding me back. I broke, my body clenching around him as he pumped in and out of me. I shouted his name, unable to keep it in while my orgasm took control, demanding more from him.

He delivered, leaning over me and letting the base of his

cock rub my clit with each stroke while he took what he needed from me.

His grunts and moans were the only sounds he made as he held my gaze from less than a foot away. Closer, I could see the stress in his jaw from holding back. He was waiting for me, wanting to see me lose control again.

And he was getting his wish.

My sensitive skin was raw and ready. It didn't take long before my body was claiming what it needed and racing to the finish. I dragged my nails down his chest as I came, spurring him on.

He leaned back again and grabbed my hips. He pulled me to him with every rough thrust inside me. He fucked me hard, demanding my body take what he was offering.

I stared at him, his mouth twisted up as if he was in pain. Every muscle was corded tight. His hands bit into my fleshy sides. He was lost, complete gone to the pleasure I was able to give to him. He couldn't stop the train racing toward him, the desire that had been building all night between us. He needed me, and I needed him.

It wouldn't last beyond tonight, but for a few minutes, we were one.

He thrust hard into me one final time and stilled. His thick cock swelled inside, then burst, the feeling muted by the condom separating us. He jerked with the release, lost in everything that happened.

I watched him the entire time, memorizing his face and the way he looked. By the time he collapsed onto me, I knew he would pretend it hadn't happened if we saw each other again. I almost wanted to cry, but I couldn't let myself when he was still there.

I laid still, waiting for him to regain his strength. When he finally pushed off me, he went straight to the bathroom.

He didn't look at me or say anything before he closed the door.

The air felt cool on my skin. I picked up my panties and slid them back on, then grabbed a robe from my closet. Before he left the bathroom, I went into the kitchen and got a glass of water.

I watched for him to return, not wanting to turn my back and hope he would do something sweet like wrap his arms around me from behind. I knew what this was. I wasn't going to romanticize it anymore than I already had.

His jeans were on and buttoned when he walked out of my room. He looked past me to where he left the rest of his clothes. He didn't say anything as he got dressed.

I set my glass in the sink and went to the door. "Thanks," I said as I unlocked it.

"Thanks?" His brows went up.

I shrugged. "What else do you want me to say?"

"You sound like you're going to slip me some cash on the way out the door."

"We both know this was a one time thing. We're adults, and this doesn't need to be awkward."

"Then why are you making it awkward?"

I shook my head. "Good night, Rowan."

He moved closer to me and stopped right in front of me. "Thanks." He hesitated, like he was going to do something like kiss me again, then opened the door. "Good night, Willow."

I forced a smile and waited until he was outside. I closed the door and leaned against it, dropping my head against the solid steel.

"Well, at least I got the cobwebs out," I told myself. I pushed away from the door and refused to get upset. It was a great night with amazing sex, for both of us. Too bad I'd never see him again.

5

ROWAN

I made it to Friday. I wasn't sure I'd make it through Friday, but I made it to Friday. I skipped O'Kelley's the night before because I was preparing for my presentation to the high schoolers. That's what I told everyone. The truth was, I wasn't looking for a fight about spending time with Willow. The town rumor mill was in full swing and I knew I would be expected to defend my actions.

My actions didn't need a defense. I did whatever the hell I wanted whenever the hell I wanted with whomever the hell I wanted. Whoever the fuck had a problem with that wasn't my damn problem.

But I knew they'd make it into a big deal, so I skipped out. And when Captain Reynolds told me to take the morning off and go straight to the school instead of coming in to the precinct, I didn't hesitate to take him up on the offer.

Which meant the first time I spoke that day was to the guard at the high school. My throat was raw from a lack of sleep and talking myself in circles while I practiced for the speech. I was not prepared.

I waited for Principal Thomas to arrive and lead me

through the school to the auditorium. I could easily find my way, but with the safety protocols in place, I wasn't pushing anything. I was in favor of anything intended to keep kids safe.

"Hello, Officer Masterson. Thanks for being here," Mrs. Thomas said with a wide grin and an extended hand.

I shook her hand and nodded, feeling less confident by the minute. I had the barebones of a talk to give and hoped the rest would come out when I opened my mouth. I still had no idea why Captain Reynolds thought I was a good fit for this talk, but I couldn't argue now. Not when I was being shown into the auditorium and introduced to a nerdy looking guy.

"Mr. Eckart will get you connected to a mic and make sure everything sounds good. I'll leave you two here, and be back in thirty minutes with the first group of students."

I nodded at her retreating back then turned my focus to Mr. Eckart.

"Thanks for doing this," he said. He held up a lapel mic. "Clip this to your collar and the battery pack can be on your belt. I'm the technology teacher."

I nodded as he handed over the device for me to attach it. When it was in place, he asked me to say something.

"Like what?" My voice echoed through the auditorium.

"That was good. I need to tune it for how you speak. Why don't you go up on stage and start your speech? It'll give me a chance to balance everything out so when the kids are here, we don't have to worry."

I nodded and did as he asked. When he told me it was good, I stopped talking and paced back and forth across the stage.

"Hey, is there a place I can get a bottle of water?"

"I'll grab you one," Mr. Eckart said. "We have some in the lounge. I'll get a few since you'll be talking a lot today."

"Thank you."

Mr Eckart left me alone in the auditorium. I mumbled to myself, trying to get the words right for the speech.

Students slammed through the auditorium doors before Mr. Eckart returned. My palms dampened and my throat seized. My heart raced and sweat beaded on my entire body. Fucking hell.

I watched as the kids filed in, shouting to their friends and shoving each other while they found seats. Teachers tried to direct them, but they were old enough that they only half listened.

Maybe that should have brought me comfort, but it made me more anxious. If they only listened to half of what I said, maybe they heard the wrong half and missed things. Maybe more people would die. Maybe—

"Here's your water, Officer Masterson," Mr. Eckart said.

I turned and looked at him, nodding my thanks and taking the bottle.

"I put a few more on the table back here in case you need them. Anything else, just ask. I'll be at the board for all your talks today. And Mrs. Thomas should be here in a minute to introduce you. Thanks again for doing this."

I nodded and hoped my throat started working before I had to begin my speech.

I sucked down the first bottle of water and grabbed a second one. I opened it but didn't drink any. It was just in case.

"Are you ready?" Mrs. Thomas asked, appearing from out of the crowd.

I nodded. "As ready as I'm gonna be."

She leaned into a microphone at the podium off to the side and said, "Good morning, students."

"Good morning, Mrs. Thomas," they said back.

"We have Officer Masterson with us today. He has volunteered to talk to everyone about spotting spirals. I ask that you give him your full attention and please listen to what he has to say. Thank you, Officer Masterson, for being here."

I nodded and stepped closer to the edge of the stage while Mrs. Thomas clapped her hands and walked off the stage. Some of the students clapped with her, but most just stared at me. Great fucking start.

"How is everyone today?" I asked them.

A few kids murmured something I construed as a positive response.

"Is anyone willing to admit they're having a crappy day?"

Someone in the middle raised his hand. I pointed at him.

"You are? Why is your day crappy?"

"Because I had a test in social studies."

The other students chuckled and murmured agreement.

"Okay. A test can definitely ruin your day. But if you study for it, and you're prepared, it's not that bad, right?"

The kid shrugged.

"Anyone else having a bad day?"

A few more hands went up. The kids told me anything from they forgot their lunch at home to they got in a fight with a friend to one twisted her ankle and couldn't play in the volleyball tournament that weekend.

"All of those things ruin your day, right? All of those things take us from here," I held my hand chest high, "to here." I lowered my hand to my waist. "They're not the worst things in the world, but they definitely make life more of a pain in the a— butt."

The students chuckled at my near-miss.

"What about things that take you lower? Things that ruin more than a day? Like the tournament. When did you hurt your ankle?" I asked the girl who'd offered the information earlier.

"Tuesday."

"Have you been practicing all week?"

She shook her head.

"And you're out of the tournament this weekend. When will you be able to practice and play again?"

She shrugged. "Hopefully next week."

"Okay, so this is something that ruins more than a day. By tomorrow, the test will be forgotten, you will have more food and the missed lunch won't be a big deal, but she's going to be dealing with this for a little more than a week. Things like that can start some people into a spiral. What if you forgot homework? It's something that would normally affect one day, right? But maybe it's the third time this month you didn't do it and you're now failing your class. Failing the class means you might not graduate on time. It means you might not be able to play the sport you want to play. It means you might get grounded or have your phone taken away. Do you see where I'm going with this? One thing, that seems little, can quickly become much bigger, especially when there's more going on."

The students nodded even though none of them said anything.

"Okay, so now that you understand how a spiral can happen, you need to know how to stop it. For the person inside, it's like a tornado. They don't know which way is out or up. They can feel the pull, and it can feel easy to give up and let it take you away. But that's not the answer. The hard thing is someone outside the spiral needs to reach for them, show them where to go, and it will all go away."

"Have you ever been in a spiral?" one student asked.

I nodded. "I have. And I've seen what happens when someone doesn't reach in and help the person trapped inside."

A few more hands went up. "Did someone die?"

The breath rushed out of me like I'd been punched.

Slowly, I nodded. I wasn't ready to share that story with a room of kids, but I knew they could feel it. They could feel the tension and the seriousness.

"How do we avoid that?" another student asked.

I forced a smile and took a sip of my water and said, "That's what we're going to talk about next."

THE REST of the talk went well. Really well. The other three were almost as good, but as the students got older, they were less interested in what I had to say. It was obvious to me the seniors already thought they knew everything. I hoped they knew enough.

Mrs. Thomas joined me on stage after my last talk. "Thank you. This was the best talk we've ever had. The students have never been so engaged. I really appreciate it. And I'll have to tell Captain Reynolds he was right to force you into this."

"Thank you, Mrs. Thomas."

She walked me to the exit after I handed my mic to Mr. Eckart and thanked him for his help. When we made it to the door, she stopped me.

"I'm sorry for your loss, Officer."

I looked at her and nodded.

"I hope you find some peace in knowing you helped these kids today."

I nodded again. "I hope I did."

She smiled. "You did. The guidance counselors have been inundated today. A lot of kids are asking for help. You did a great thing for these students. Thank you."

I nodded and thanked her again, then walked out into the bright afternoon. The air was still and the sun was bright, and if it weren't hovering around ten degrees, it would have been a nice day. The kind of day Sanders used to say was a gift from God.

It had been far too long since I'd reached out to his ex-wife. Beverly welcomed me into her home and her world when I started working with Sanders. I watched as their marriage changed and fell apart, and as he fell apart shortly after.

"Rowan?" she asked when she answered the phone.

"Hi, Beverly. How are you?"

"Holy shit, Rowan. How are you? Where are you?"

"I'm in a tiny town called MacKellar Cove. It's in upstate New York."

"Are you okay?"

I shrugged and drew a deep breath. "As okay as I can be. I was thinking about you. Wanted to check in. How are you?"

"Pretty much the same as always," she said with a mirthless laugh.

"How's Tony?" I asked.

"Pretty much the same as always. He misses you."

"I miss him, too."

"When are you coming back?"

I sighed. "I haven't heard yet. Six months to a year was the original agreement. I should get an update soon."

"I still don't think they should have asked you to take time off. You didn't do anything wrong."

"We both know I did, Bev. If I hadn't, he would still be here."

She tsked and said, "We both know that isn't true. He wanted to be gone, so he's gone. I hate it for Tony, but my ex-husband made the choices that put him in the position he was in at the end. If he couldn't see a way out and couldn't accept that he needed help, there was nothing anyone could have done to change that."

"I wish I could see it that way."

"You should. And hopefully one day you will. I loved him once, but he changed. When you find someone, make sure she knows who you are inside and out. Don't hide things from her. And for God's sake, don't lie to her about your job. We all need someone in our lives who has our backs. For some of us, it's a spouse or significant other, for some, it's a friend or relative, but we all need someone we can go to no matter what. When you find that person, let them in."

My breath hitched. I nodded. I thought I had that person in Sanders. He was a mentor in ways I never realized. John taught me how to be a better cop and how to be a better man. I never thought he would also teach me how to deal with loss.

"So, have you met someone up there?" Beverly asked. She was constantly trying to fix me up with women she knew. I dated a few of them, but none of them clicked.

"No," I said firmly. Too quickly.

"Tell me about her," Beverly insisted.

"There's no one and nothing to tell."

"Then it shouldn't be a problem to share it, Rowan. If you've found even an ounce of joy through all this, then good for you. You deserve it. And if there's one thing I knew about John, he wouldn't want the rest of us to blame ourselves and limit our joy because he lost his."

"It doesn't feel right to be happy. Like I don't deserve it because he's not here."

"Millions of people aren't here, Rowan. Everyone has lost someone. If we stopped living because someone else did, none of us would exist. We'd have died out centuries ago."

I chuckled at her twisted logic and admitted she was right.

"So, tell me about her."

"There really isn't anything to tell," I said, even as Willow's face popped into my head. The way she responded to me the other night and the feistiness in her eyes…I was having a hard time pushing her out of my mind. "She's…I've been told to stay away from her."

Beverly laughed loudly. "Say no more. Now I understand why you like her. No one can tell Rowan Masterson what to do."

I grumbled but she was right. The idea that Willow was off limits made her that much more appealing to me. A mystery I wanted to solve. One night with her wasn't nearly enough. I wanted more.

"It sounds like you enjoy her company."

"She can't stand me."

Beverly laughed again. "I like her already."

"I gave her a ticket. She ripped me a new one for it."

"Did you tear it up?"

"Hell, no. She was parked illegally. In a loading zone."

Beverly snorted. "You always followed the letter of the law."

"I am a cop. If I'm not going to, how can I expect anyone else to."

"Well, this woman will come around. She'll learn to love you. One day."

"I like seeing her smile. I like making her smile," I admitted.

"Aw. That's quite possibly the best goal you can have."

Beverly and I spoke a few more minutes before she said she needed to get Tony ready for basketball practice. I promised to call again and to update her as soon as I heard something.

I hoped that was soon. But maybe not too soon.

6

I was feeling good about the presentations and wanted to get out and celebrate a little. I'd taken to walking all over town since my only transportation was a motorcycle. It was great through the summer, but with winter in full swing, I was wishing I had something with a roof.

O'Kelley's was wall to wall people when I made it through the door. A Friday night always brought a crowd, and Hudson told me in November that he was busier in the winter than the summer. Something about locals who stick around and like to drink since there was nothing else to do in MacKellar Cove when it was so cold. I thought he was joking.

I pushed my way to the bar and managed to catch Hudson's attention. He nodded and kept working until he could bring a beer over to me.

"It's nuts in here," I said.

He nodded. "Welcome to January. I told you November wasn't bad compared to this."

"It's insane. How the hell do you keep up?"

"Lots of help," he said as Piper walked by with a tray loaded with drinks and food. "Good help."

"That's for sure."

"Were you hiding last night?"

"Hiding?" I asked, trying to pretend I had no idea what he was talking about. How could he possibly have known?

"Yeah. After you met up with Willow twice this week, I imagine Ramsey is looking to have a chat."

I snorted and shook my head. "I'm not afraid of Ramsey. Between you and Rucker, I've been warned."

"But you're not listening," Hudson said, eyeing me closely.

I sipped my beer and ignored the statement that was really a question. "I'll be here next week."

"Uh huh. We'll see."

I rolled my eyes. I was not afraid of any of them. I'd faced far worse than the worst MacKellar Cove could throw at me, and I lived to tell about it. Ramsey didn't scare me.

"I think Gavin is here somewhere," Hudson said. "If you're looking for someone to talk to besides Willow."

I nodded and refused to take the bait and ask if Willow was there. Hudson waited until I shook my head then walked away laughing.

I looked around the bar for Gavin, not Willow, but didn't spot either of them. Deciding to hang on to the stool where I was, I dug out my phone and checked for anything I missed.

Before I pulled anything up, someone jostled me from behind. "Sorry," she said, resting her hand on my back. She let it linger and waited for me to turn to look at her.

"Not a problem," I said.

She smiled and leaned closer. "It's impossible to get a drink right now. I see you have one."

I nodded and lifted it. "I do."

"Do you mind if I squeeze right in here with you and see if I can get someone's attention?"

"Sure," I said, shifting over enough to let her stand next to me.

"I'm Marnie, by the way."

I shook her hand. "Rowan."

"Nice. Are you a local?"

I nodded. "Of sorts."

"Me, too. I moved here over the summer. I'm not so sure about the winter. It's really cold." She shivered, pushing her breasts forward.

"I hear drinking is the only thing to do around here all winter," I told her.

She laughed one of those fake, loud laughs that was designed to catch the attention of everyone around. I forced a smile for her and sipped my drink.

Hudson walked over and narrowed his eyes at me in question. I shrugged. I didn't know her either.

"What can I get you?" he asked Marnie.

"Oh, yay. Thank you. Finally. Um, I need a Screaming Orgasm. And since this guy hasn't given me one yet, I'll take one from you."

I choked on my beer. Hudson barely even blinked. He nodded and walked away, leaving me to deal with her.

"Excuse me?" I asked her.

She shrugged and leaned closer, putting her too perky boobs on my arm. "Want to get out of here?"

"Hey, man!" Gavin said, appearing out of nowhere. "I was looking for you. Your girlfriend is at our table."

"Girlfriend?" Marnie asked. "You didn't tell me you had a girlfriend."

I shrugged. "I didn't realize I needed to until now."

"Grab your beer. Let's go," Gavin said, nodding toward the other side of the bar.

I squeezed my way past Marnie, trying not to touch her again. She was a pretty enough woman, but she was trying way too hard. If a woman needed to ask a man for a screaming orgasm as her pick up line, she was definitely trying too hard.

As soon as we were out of earshot I thanked Gavin for the rescue.

"Hudson told me you were being accosted. That woman is determined."

I nodded. "Yeah. I was not prepared for her."

Gavin threw his arm around my shoulders and led me to the back where he did indeed have a table. Piper was standing next to it, talking to Willow.

"Willow?" I hissed.

Gavin shrugged. "I don't have loyalties either. And Piper said she's nice. I'd rather get laid and piss off Ramsey than miss out on sex with my woman."

I sighed and let Gavin lead me the rest of the way to the table. When Willow saw me walking toward her with Gavin, she tensed.

"What are you doing here?" she asked.

"I had to rescue him from a vulture at the bar," Gavin said. "She was trying to swallow him whole right there on a bar stool."

"You should have let her. He probably deserves it for something," Willow said. She crossed her arms and leaned back in her chair.

"Um, I need to get back to work. Play nice," Piper said.

Gavin wrapped his arms around her and drew her in for a slow kiss while I took a seat next to Willow.

"I didn't expect to see you here tonight," I told her.

She shrugged. "I didn't realize I wasn't allowed to be here when I felt like it."

"That's not what I meant."

"Did you mean I should call you before I do anything? That I should clear my schedule with you?" She dug her phone out of her purse and typed something into it. I watched her, resisting the urge to laugh. Not many people stood toe-to-toe with me. But she didn't back down. Ever.

My phone buzzed in my pocket, and I pulled it out without thinking. When I saw a notification from the Book Boyfriends Wanted app, I opened it.

Then I did laugh.

UPFORANYTHING

Spending time at O'Kelley's tonight. Is that okay with you?

Instead of looking up, I replied to her in the app.

JUSTVISITING

Sounds good. Maybe I can buy you a drink. Vodka, right?

I set my phone on the table facedown and met her gaze. Her phone buzzed and she glared at me before she broke eye contact and looked at it.

She pulled her bottom lip between her teeth, just the edge, and typed a response.

UPFORANYTHING

Will you buy two? So I can throw one in your face.

I barked a laugh and shook my head.

JUSTVISITING

That might sting a little. How about a shot you can lick off me?

Her eyes widened when she read my message. She glanced up at me from beneath her lashes without moving her head, trying not to get caught. Then she replied.

UPFORANYTHING

That's probably not a good idea.

JUSTVISITING

If you change your mind, you know how to get in touch with me.

She nodded and slid her phone back into her purse, then picked up her drink. She drained it then stood. "I need another."

"I can grab it for you," Piper said. She was still trying to tear herself away from Gavin, and failing.

Willow shook her head. "I need to head to the bathroom, too. And I don't need babysitters all night."

"We're not babysitters. Friends," Gavin said.

Willow forced a smile and eased her way around the table, giving me plenty of space like I'd done with Marnie. I watched her go, letting my gaze linger on her ass until the crowd swallowed her up.

"So, the guys weren't kidding when they said you're playing with fire," Gavin said, taking the seat Willow vacated.

I shook my head. "And I thought you said you don't have loyalties."

Gavin leaned back and held up his hands. "I'm innocent, Officer." He chuckled.

"There's nothing going on with us. She's less than interested."

"That's not what it looked like to me."

I shook my head. "Trust me."

Gavin shrugged and avoided my gaze for a minute. He looked out at the crowd, then he leaned forward again. "Things aren't always what they seem."

I chuckled. "And sometimes, they're exactly how they seem. Willow isn't interested, and the guys are wrong. I'm not playing with fire."

"What were you sexting her?"

I coughed. "What?"

Gavin snickered. "I thought so. I know sexting when I see it."

"You could see?"

Gavin snorted. "Nope, but you just admitted it. And it was written all over your faces. I don't think she knows how to handle you. From what Piper told me, she doesn't have a lot of people in her corner. If you want to be, show her you're here for her."

"You make it sound like I'm trying to get her to go steady. I'm not looking to get attached to anyone."

"You're not staying, are you?"

"What?" I breathed.

Gavin leaned in closer. "You're not sticking around. You're leaving. You only plan to be here for a while, then you're going back to your life, wherever it is. That's why you don't want to get involved."

"No, I...how the hell did you figure that out?"

Gavin breathed a laugh. "Because I did the same thing. I told myself Piper was a fling, a holiday or vacation fling. She was my version of a summer girl, but in the winter. I came here every summer as a kid, and I had a girl most summers that I spent time with, but I was always leaving. I'd go home, and I always told them we'd stay in touch, but we didn't. When I met Piper, I thought she would be the same, because I was scared of getting attached to this place. I loved it here growing up, but I convinced myself I wanted a busier life, a faster pace. But none of that was true."

"You had a life, though, right?"

Gavin nodded. "I did, but it was an empty one. I worked

and I played soccer with friends once in a while, but I didn't have anyone in my corner, someone to be there for me. I didn't have someone that made me want to rush home from work. Now, I do."

"I've never known that. I don't even know if I want it."

Gavin chuckled. "Trust me. You do."

He stood and nodded once, then headed toward the bar. If I had to guess, he was going to look for Piper and steal another kiss from her.

I nursed my beer and debated leaving the table. It was hard to find one, but if I was the only one sitting there, why did we need it?

I nodded hello to a few people I'd met in town and returned a few dirty looks from people I didn't know. When a young couple who were barely able to stand asked if they could sit down, I decided it was time to give up the table and find my way out of there.

Gavin was parked on a bar stool near the kitchen, likely so he could talk to Piper whenever she walked by. I didn't spot Willow at all, but something told me she was still there.

On my way to Gavin, I was stopped by someone I let out of a ticket the week before.

"Hey, man, let me buy you a drink," the guy said.

"I was just on my way out."

"I owe you, though. Letting me out of that ticket was major. You are a rock star, sir."

I nodded at his drunk ass and debated what I should do. "How are you getting home tonight?"

"Walking, dude. I don't drink and drive. We're all walking. We don't live far. See, that's what I mean. You're awesome!"

I forced a smile and tried not to be bothered by his beer breath when he threw his arm around me and led me toward the bar. He raised his other arm and got the attention of the bartender. "A drink for my friend, for not giving me a ticket and giving me a second chance."

"You did what?" came from behind me.

I spun away from the drunk guy and faced Willow. She had her arms crossed below her plump chest, lifting her breasts up. Fire sparked in her brown eyes. If I was a betting man, I'd say she was going to hit me. Soon.

"Oh, he's awesome. He was going to give me a ticket, but I saw him. I asked him not to write it, and he didn't. It's he great?"

"Yeah, really great. He's the best," Willow said, sarcasm and anger dripping from her words.

"Willow," I tried.

She held her hands up and backed away. "Don't. Seriously, just don't. You don't owe me anything."

"Dammit," I swore as she headed straight for the door.

My new best friend threw his arm around me again and brought a beer up in front of me. I took it and thanked him, watching Willow retreat the entire time.

One sip of the beer, and the guy cheered. All his friends joined in. They slid back into the crowd and all but vanished just as Willow made it to the door.

She didn't look back. The door slammed behind her, telling me how pissed off she was. That fire...fucking hell she got to me. I couldn't let her walk away alone. Even if she hated me, I wanted her, and I was going to be a gentleman, dammit.

I set the beer on the bar and pushed my way through the crowd, hoping to catch her before she got too far. She lived to the left, so I went that way, spotting her a few yards away. I hurried to get to her and fell into step beside her.

She glanced my way and rolled her eyes. "What the hell do you want?"

"I'm just walking you home."

"I can take care of myself."

I nodded. "I'm sure you can."

She looked at me like I was crazy then kept walking. She didn't tell me to leave her alone, so I kept going with her. Maybe it was going to be a good night.

7

WILLOW

I did not want him to walk me home again. He let some guy out of a ticket but he gave me one. What the hell? If he knew who I was and gave me a ticket on purpose, why was he spending time with me?

"Am I a joke to you? A bet? Something like that?" I asked, whirling on him on the sidewalk.

He stopped quickly, almost running into me when I stopped. He shook his head. "You really think I'd do something like that?"

I shrugged. "I don't know you. I don't know anything about you. We had sex once, and we kissed, and we've never had a conversation. How do I know that's not exactly who you are?"

He shook his head and took a step back. "I'm not like that, Willow. I like you. You challenge me, and you confuse me. You make me want to do new things and give people a chance. I don't know you, but I like what I do know. Spending time with you is not a joke or a bet or a trick or whatever else you're thinking. I'm getting more shit for it than anything else."

"So, you knew from the beginning who I was. You put that ticket on my car because it was my car?"

He chuckled and shook his head. "I put that ticket on your car because you were parked in a loading zone. And the truck was waiting for you to move."

"What about the other guy?"

"The guy in the bar?"

"Yeah, the guy who said you're so awesome because you didn't give him a ticket."

He sighed. "His meter expired. He was on his way to put money in it when I was about to write the ticket. I'm a reasonable guy."

"Not for me."

"Really? You were inside for at least ten minutes, blocking that truck. If you were on your way out, I wouldn't have given you a ticket. Hell, if the truck wasn't waiting on you, I might not have given you the ticket."

"Whatever."

I started to walk away again. I wasn't interested in his excuses or explanations. He raced to catch up to me.

"Are you mad at me about a ticket or is it something else? Because I feel like there's something else going on."

"It's nothing."

"Really? Then why are you storming away from a night out and acting like I cheated on you with your best friend."

"Why are you here? Why are you acting like you care about me?" I asked.

"Maybe I do," he said softly. "Why is it so hard for you to let me?"

I looked up at him. "I don't do messy things like emotions. Not anymore. I learned my lesson."

"Then this doesn't need to be about emotions. It can just be about sex."

The low timbre of his voice slid down my spine like

honey. Slow, sticking to every inch of me, and forcing me to pay attention to exactly what he wanted.

"I can handle that," I said. I didn't need a connection. I didn't need emotions. I didn't need a man who was going to try to take care of me.

I also didn't believe my own lies, but a fragile connection was better than no connection at all.

We didn't speak again until we made it to my apartment. He pressed himself to my back while I unlocked my door. His lips were on my neck as we moved inside. His hands touched my bare skin, already stripping me naked as we fought to shut the cold out.

There was nothing slow about our movements. I tugged at his pants while he shoved my jacket off my shoulders. I pushed him back while he tried to cup my breasts. We fought each other's movements the entire time.

And we watched. We stared at each other, our eyes devouring the other's body. His abs came into view, then his chest, teasing me and soaking my panties as he flexed his muscles to remove his shirt. He bent to untie his boots, turning to give me a spectacular view of his ass.

I couldn't resist running my hand over his ass and trailing my fingertips up his spine. He stilled at my touch, then stood and pressed me hard against my door. His tongue was in my mouth before I could take another breath. His naked upper body was hot against mine, my bra the only barrier between us.

Not for long.

He cupped my breasts and tugged the cups to the side with his thumbs, rasping both over my greedy nipples. I gasped and bit his tongue. He pulled back and dragged his lips down my neck. He lifted my breasts to his lips, closing his teeth around one.

I moaned, loving the bite of pain that sent a jolt of pleasure through me. He sucked hard, bringing another sensation to the forefront, then flicked my nipple with his tongue.

I worked to release the clasp on my bra while he teased me, groaning when I couldn't get one hook to open. He grinned against my flesh at my frustration, then pressed my nipple to the roof of his mouth and I no longer cared about anything else.

I bought my hands to his head and held him in place. He drew more of my breast into his mouth then released it with a soft pop. He blew on my wet nipple, igniting all my senses.

"Oh, God," I moaned softly, needing more of him.

While he moved to the other nipple, I fought to get my bra off, nearly cheering when it released and I could drop it to the floor. He tormented my other nipple then buried his face between my breasts and nipped at the tender flesh on the inside of each.

"More," I begged him.

"Take the rest of your clothes off. Now," he commanded.

I did as he asked, dropping my pants to the ground and kicking off my boots. He pulled out a condom then lost his pants and boxer briefs. He rolled the condom on quickly and pulled me close to him again. He kissed me, a kiss that was less gentle and more demanding than anything. But it was what I needed. It was perfect. Because we weren't building something. We weren't falling for each other. We were having sex.

And I needed that reminder.

He guided us to my bedroom and kissed me while our hands roamed each other's bodies. I traced his muscles with my fingertips, loving the way they jumped at my touch. He pulled me in closer when I ran my nails down his back. And when I threaded my fingers through his hair, he groaned and kissed me harder.

My knees started to give out when he slid a hand between

us and entered me with two thick fingers. I was wet and ready for him, unable to hide how much I wanted him. The feeling was mutual if the erection digging into my stomach was anything to go by.

His hand stayed between my thighs while he guided me to lay on the bed. He stroked me gently, teasing my body with light brushes over my clit and slow thrusts inside. I wanted more at the same time that I wanted him to keep doing the same thing.

Until he thrust his fingers hard into me, and my entire body splintered.

"Oh, God, Rowan. Yes! Yes!"

He groaned with me and withdrew his hand to my whimpers.

"No, please. More," I begged him, reaching for him.

The bed dipped and his cock rubbed the overly sensitive flesh between my thighs. In one smooth stroke, he thrust deep inside, setting off mini-aftershocks that made my fingers and toes tingle.

"Yes," I groaned as he began to move. More and more, the feelings ignited in me. My body was on fire, flames licking at my skin every time our bodies met.

I looked up at him, wanting to see the look on his face. His eyes were closed. His jaw clenched tight. His mouth pinched, with a slight opening between his lips. Breath rushed out of him with every thrust, like he was trying to hold it back and couldn't. His biceps were tense, fighting every instinct to let go and collapse.

He could have been the poster boy for great sex. It was written all over his face. The intensity. The desire. The passion.

And it was all for me.

I couldn't keep my own desire in check with his on display like that. I tried to hold back and let him have it all, let him enjoy the moment, but it was too overwhelming. It raced through me like the fire I felt was real. What started in my fingertips and toes licked up my arms and legs and settled in my core. My whole body burned from head to toe as my orgasm washed over me, blazing like a wildfire.

I shouted with surprise at the powerful sensation, then grabbed Rowan, needing him to ground me. To remind me I wasn't alone.

I never lost my mind during sex. I never had an orgasm sneak up on me. But I never slept with a man like Rowan. A man who made me feel things I didn't want to feel and made me want things I shouldn't want to want.

But I did. He was there and he was making it impossible for those messy feelings to stay inside. Letting them out always meant danger. It always meant things got ugly. But when he shouted my name and pulsed inside me, I wasn't sure I could hold them back.

He collapsed onto me, whispering words I couldn't understand. He kissed my neck and nibbled at my jaw. When he finally pushed off me, he avoided my gaze and disappeared into my bathroom like last time.

A wave of regret hit me hard. I'd just had the best sex of my life, and he was acting like it was the same as every day. It was those damn emotions I told myself not to let out.

I got dressed while he finished in the bathroom. When he walked out, he barely glanced at me before he found his clothes. He stopped before he pulled his shirt over his head and just looked at me. His gaze slid from my toes to my eyes and back down again.

I waited for whatever he wanted to say, bracing myself for it.

"This might be about more than just sex for me, Willow. I know you don't want emotions, but I just wanted you to know that."

I opened my mouth to respond, but I didn't know what I wanted to say. I snapped it shut, and he nodded once, then left my bedroom.

I followed him, wondering what to say, and realized I had to tell him the truth. "I might feel the same."

He looked at me and nodded once. "I'll talk to you soon."

I nodded and waited for him to kiss me or something, but he just walked out the door.

Guess I wasn't the only one who sucked with emotions.

8

———

ROWAN

I didn't see Willow again for a week. I barely saw anyone. I was focused on work and hadn't been out much. I told myself that was why I braved O'Kelley's with Rucker and his friends. It was not because I was trying to prove I wasn't afraid of Ramsey and the rest of them. Or because I was hoping to run into Willow.

I might have amended that thought when I made it to the bar. I took a seat next to Ian, glancing around to see if Willow was there, and was immediately attacked.

"Why the hell are you talking to the evil seed?"

"What were you thinking leaving with her?"

"Why? Just why?"

I should have expected it but that whole small town thing was still sinking in. When Hudson set a glass of whiskey in front of me, I looked up at him. He stood back with his arms crossed over his chest and his eyebrows raised expectantly. Of course he was the one who told them all I was talking to Willow.

"Since when do any of you care what I do?"

64

"Since she tried to ruin my marriage. And almost did," Ramsey said.

"Look, I get it. You don't like her, but why does that mean I can't?"

The rest of them leaned back and sucked in a breath, then ducked their heads and glanced at Ramsey. He glared at me, a combination of shock and anger on his face.

"She told my wife that I was in love with her. That I only proposed because I couldn't handle my attraction to her and was settling. She manipulated Melody for years to try to end our marriage. She's a horrible person."

"Were you?"

"Was I what?"

"In love with her."

Ramsey's brows shot up, but from the curious looks the other men gave him, it was a question no one had bothered to ask. One Ramsey had never bothered to answer.

"No," Ramsey said when he realized no one was going to answer for him. He sighed. "She was Melody's kid sister. I thought she was sweet, but I never thought of her as anything other than Mel's little sister. When she kissed me… it threw me off. But I didn't choose Mel because Willow was too young. I chose Melody because she's the only woman I've ever loved. I chose her because I wanted to spend the rest of my life with her. I still do. Every day I wake up thankful she's in my life."

"Okay, so if you don't love Willow, why can't I get to know her?"

Ramsey shook his head. "Listen, I'm trying to watch out for you. She's bad news. My wife has been in tears more times than I can count because of Willow. She was supposed to be Melody's best friend, and instead, she turned out to be her worst enemy. She took everything she knew about us, about

Melody, and used it to try to end our relationship. Because she had some misguided crush on me and thought I felt the same. If you really want to get to know her, I can't stop you, but I want you to know the kind of person you're talking to."

"Got it," I said. I sipped my whiskey. "I make my own mistakes."

"None as big as this one," Rucker muttered under his breath.

If he only knew. But I didn't correct him. I didn't correct any of them. My past wasn't a part of my story in MacKellar Cove. No one was going to know the real reason I was there, or that I was leaving as soon as I was allowed to return to my home.

I was in town to keep myself out of trouble and to wait for internal affairs to decide my future. The fact that it was going to take up to a year for everything to happen was not something I was going to dwell on.

"Is anything else going on in this town besides me making friends with the evil seed?" I asked, hoping to redirect the conversation to someone else.

"I'm getting closer to talking my sister into moving up here," Gavin said. "She keeps saying she has to wait for the kids to finish the school year. She's talking about spending some of the summer here, and I'm hoping she'll remember how much she loves it."

"How does Sebastian feel about that?" Rucker asked.

Gavin shrugged. "I haven't talked to him much. He's keeping his distance from us."

"How did none of us know there was something between them?" Ian asked.

I wasn't up on all the history, but it made me feel better that the history was spotty for the rest of them. Gavin seemed like a good guy, and his sister was nice. A little shy and unsure of herself, but Gavin shared she'd just gone through a divorce and was still raw from the end of her marriage.

"Zoey told me she thought everyone knew. When we used to come here, we sort of kept to ourselves. I mean, we were around, but there was a difference between us and the rest of you," Gavin said.

"Yeah, because you weren't a local. You were one of the summer kids," Ramsey said. "When we were in high school and worked, it was nice to have extra people around to make some money, but it also sucked to watch people like you living it up and we had to do a job all day."

"I worked, too. I just worked at the Inn. Aunt Gina made sure we were done by midday so we could enjoy some time off," Gavin explained. He shrugged and sipped his beer. Another one appeared in front of him as he set the bottle down. He looked over his shoulder with a grin.

"Where's mine?" Ian asked.

Piper laughed and shook her head. "It's coming."

"She likes me best," Gavin said with a nod and a smirk.

"I'm okay with that," Ian replied. "As long as I get another beer, too."

Piper chuckled and set the rest of the drinks in front of us. She held her tray against her side and went back to Gavin's side. "Need anything else?"

Gavin tilted his head up and pulled her closer. "Yep."

Piper grinned and wrapped her free arm around Gavin as he pulled her in for a kiss.

I didn't mean to intrude on their moment, but watching them made me think of Willow. She was always looking around when she was at O'Kelley's, like she was waiting for someone to kick her out. She was never as comfortable as Piper was.

Then again, I wasn't going to slide my hand to her ass in public and kiss her like I was starved the way Gavin was doing with Piper. Although I wouldn't pass up the chance to kiss Willow like that again.

Gavin finally let Piper up for air. She blushed and licked her lips, bringing the bottom one between her teeth. He said something I couldn't hear, and she nodded.

I'd never had that kind of comfort with another person. That connection. Maybe I was reaching, but there was something about Willow that made me think I could have it with her. If I was sticking around.

Which I wasn't, so it didn't matter.

THE GUYS MADE it an early night, and after working so much, I was not interested in going home. I needed a break. I needed a woman. I needed Willow.

I didn't have her number, so I opened the Book Boyfriends Wanted app and pulled up her information.

JUSTVISITING

Hey, are you home?

UPFORANYTHING

Um, yeah. Why?

JUSTVISITING

I'm coming over.

UPFORANYTHING

How do you know where I live?

JUSTVISITING

I've been there. With you. This is Rowan.

UPFORANYTHING

I'm busy.

JUSTVISITING

Doing what?

UPFORANYTHING

None of your business.

JUSTVISITING

I'm coming over.

UPFORANYTHING

I haven't heard from you since you walked out my door. I've moved on.

Ouch. That stung.

JUSTVISITING

I don't believe you.

UPFORANYTHING

Doesn't matter. It's true.

JUSTVISITING

You know I can find out anything I want to know about you.

UPFORANYTHING

That's an abuse of your power.

JUSTVISITING

Nope. It's small town living. There are plenty of people willing to tell me anything I want to know about you. Some of them were talking to me tonight.

UPFORANYTHING

About what?

JUSTVISITING

Open your door and I'll tell you.

UPFORANYTHING

You're here?

I knocked on her door to prove it.

UPFORANYTHING

I told you I'm busy!

JUSTVISITING

Open the door, Willow.

I waited, straining to listen to her inside the apartment. When the lock turned and she opened the door just enough to peek out, I put my phone away. "Are you going to let me in?"

"No."

I chuckled. "Why not?"

"Because I'm busy."

The opening song for *The Office* played loudly behind her. I raised an eyebrow, letting her know I knew she was full of shit.

"You don't want to know what people are saying about you?"

She shook her head. "Nope. I already know. Don't bother. Stay away. She's not worth it. She's a liar and a horrible person, and you're better off if you don't get involved. I don't need you to tell me they said it."

"They don't know me. I don't back down. And I don't listen to what others have to say about someone."

She smiled sadly and nodded. "Well, I guess that's good. Thanks for stopping by."

She started to close her door, but I stuck my foot in the way. "When can I see you again?"

She chuckled. "Probably in another week when you decide you need more sex. For tonight, I'm going inside. Alone."

I wanted to argue with her, but she closed the door before I had a chance.

I couldn't deny I loved a challenge.

I SENT Willow messages on Book Boyfriends Wanted all weekend. They ranged from asking what she was doing to asking what she was wearing.

She ignored me a few times, but she always responded eventually. Usually with something sarcastic. She was making it tough for me to resist her, especially when she messaged me late Sunday night.

UPFORANYTHING

Have you ever gotten excited about something that wasn't sexual at all, but it made you all horny?

My cock twitched at her words.

JUSTVISITING

I'm experiencing it right now. Then again, you said horny, so maybe it doesn't apply.

UPFORANYTHING

LOL. I mean something innocent, but knowing about it gets you all excited.

JUSTVISITING

See my previous statement.

UPFORANYTHING

You're useless. Maybe I should go talk to someone else.

JUSTVISITING

Don't you dare woman.

UPFORANYTHING

You don't get to tell me what to do.

JUSTVISITING

Next time.

UPFORANYTHING

Can I ask you something?

JUSTVISITING

Sure.

UPFORANYTHING

Why are you still talking to me?

JUSTVISITING

Because I want to.

UPFORANYTHING

You know I won't be offended if you just disappear one day.

JUSTVISITING

Good to know, but I have no plans to do that. I need a chance to tell you what to do.

UPFORANYTHING

Is that what you like? Being in charge?

JUSTVISITING

It depends. I don't mind a woman bossing me around once in a while.

UPFORANYTHING

Wow, that's a shock.

I chuckled and shook my head.

JUSTVISITING

It has to be a fair thing. I'm a fan of fair. And doing things in kind. Like if I have a taste, I'm not going to tell her she can't.

UPFORANYTHING

Now I get it.

JUSTVISITING

Get what?

UPFORANYTHING

You only go down on a woman if you know she's going to suck you off.

I choked on my water and spewed it all over myself.

JUSTVISITING

Not what I meant. You just made me spit on myself.

UPFORANYTHING

You must be really flexible. I just heard about a yoga studio in town. Want to take a class?

I laughed out loud at her and shook my head again. I'd never known a woman who could make me laugh. In Phoenix, I spent most of my time moving from one woman to the next without pausing to figure out if they had much of a personality. If they started to get attached, I was gone, but most of the time I didn't stick around long enough for them to even think about getting attached anyway.

But Willow...I couldn't explain her if I tried. She had a backbone and a hard side. She wasn't willing to back down from anything. She was definitely not my type at all. A little loud and brash. She didn't even try to blend in with the crowd. She looked like she wanted to piss everyone off.

Unless you looked into her eyes. In the depths, you saw the fight. She wanted to push them away before they rejected her. Didn't she know by now that I was not going to say no to her?

JUSTVISITING

Not what I meant, but sure I'll take a class with you. I'm assuming you're going, too.

UPFORANYTHING

Seriously?

JUSTVISITING

Yeah, why not. Don't women wear tight clothes to do yoga? You have to be in front of me so I can check out your ass.

UPFORANYTHING

Yeah, right. Nothing good to look at there.

JUSTVISITING

Well, it sure felt good. How about we try out some naked yoga sometime?

UPFORANYTHING

Do you think about anything other than sex?

JUSTVISITING

Nope.

UPFORANYTHING

At least you're honest.

JUSTVISITING

Lies aren't good for anyone.

UPFORANYTHING

I learned that lesson the hard way.

JUSTVISITING

Oh yeah, how's that?

I knew the answer, but I wanted her to tell me about it. Hearing from Ramsey and Hudson and Rucker about Willow was nothing like hearing from Willow. She had her side of the story, and I wanted to hear it before I believed what everyone else said.

UPFORANYTHING

Sorry, I need to go.

JUSTVISITING

Seriously?

UPFORANYTHING

Yep. I'll let you know about yoga. If you're really interested.

JUSTVISITING

Regular yoga and naked yoga. Yes to both.

UPFORANYTHING

LOL. We'll see.

JUSTVISITING

Looking forward to it.

She signed off the app before I sent the last message. I hoped she told me about yoga, not because I loved it, but because real yoga might lead to naked yoga, and I was all in for that.

Speaking of which, I needed a cold shower.

9

WILLOW

$\mathcal{A}$ new yoga studio. I never thought I'd see it anywhere near my town. It was exciting and a little scary. I'd thought about opening one, but I didn't have the money and didn't know anything about running a business. And the one person I knew who did was not speaking to me.

But I could take classes and I could be a member and I could learn what I could and hopefully it would translate into more experience for when I found another job some-where that wasn't MacKellar Cove.

I was sure Rowan was joking about taking a class with me, but when I mentioned I would be at the one Tuesday night, he said he'd join me. Even bigger shock was that he showed up.

"You have to promise you won't laugh at me," he said as we found spots in class.

I shook my head. "I make no promises of that nature."

He grinned and my insides did funny things.

I didn't want to like him. Yeah, the sex was spectacular, but he was a cop. And he was friends with Ramsey. The fact that he was still speaking to me was enough of a shock and made me wonder if he was a spy, but the way his eyes lingered on my curves and the way his sweatpants bulged in the front...I was pretty sure his ulterior motives had nothing to do with my brother-in-law.

He laid the hot pink mat I brought for him on the ground. When I handed it over, he raised an eyebrow but didn't make a comment. I was sure he would refuse to use it and had a black one in my car just in case, but he took it like a man and embraced his feminine side. Or so he said.

He could embrace my feminine side.

I put my lavender mat next to his and sat down to remove my socks. He looked at me then folded onto his mat, looking less than comfortable.

"Are you sure I should be here?"

"You're the one who said you wanted to come."

"Always, but I don't know anything about yoga."

I rolled my eyes at his pun and said, "There are newbies in every class. You'll pick it up. And if you don't, it'll be fodder for later."

He chuckled softly and shook his head.

The instructor moved to the front of the class and welcomed us. She went through a brief intro about the studio and herself, thanking everyone for trying out a class. She turned on music and dimmed the lights and began.

All my stress filtered away.

I followed along with the instructor and owner of Balanced Life, Sylvia, and felt so at ease. She had a soft voice and a calming presence that melted over me and made me feel like I could do anything. That was what I loved about yoga. I was limitless. Yes, I needed to work to perfect a pose or maximize a stretch, but I was always able to do something that helped my body.

Rowan, on the other hand, didn't seem to feel the same way.

More than once during class, he swore under his breath. He fell over, and he grunted a few times. Sylvia was helping another attendee at one point, so I went over to Rowan and helped him get into the right position.

"If you open your hips, this is easier. Try it like that," I said softly.

He grunted his thanks and nodded.

The next time he was struggling, he asked me to help him. I became his personal instructor while Sylvia guided the class. I showed Rowan a few alternative moves for some of the harder poses since he was obviously the only newbie there.

Sylvia saw me helping him but never interrupted us, so I figured she was okay with it. I wasn't trying to overstep, but I also had a feeling Rowan was feeling self conscious about his inability to move the way the rest of us were.

When Sylvia made it to sun salutations, Rowan groaned. I shot him a look and hissed, "What is wrong with you?"

He looked down, leading my gaze to his tented sweatpants. My eyes widened.

"What the hell?"

"You're wearing tight clothes and bending in all kinds of ways. Touching me and shit. What do you expect?"

My entire body burned at his words. The look in his eyes said he was not joking. He was hard as hell because of me.

"Tell me we're almost done."

I nodded and focused on the movements instead of on Rowan. I tried to. He grunted and groaned his way through them all, his tones low enough that I was likely the only one who heard him.

When we finished and moved into the cool down and rest

period before the session ended, Rowan looked over at me. "My place or yours?"

I grinned and shook my head, but we both knew naked yoga was next on the agenda. My panties were soaked, and it wasn't because I was sweating so much.

Rowan rolled up his mat and accepted the praise from the rest of the people in class. They told him they hoped to see him again on their way out, the way most yogis did when a new person joined.

I slid our mats into my bags and was about to leave with him when Sylvia approached us.

"You know your stuff," she said to me. "I'm Sylvia."

"Nice to meet you. I'm Willow."

"Where have you trained?"

I shook my head. "Nowhere really. I do a lot of yoga online since there isn't, or wasn't, a studio in the area. This is great."

"Thanks. I've been wanting to do this for a long time, but I was raising my kids. The last one graduated from high school last year, and I told my husband it was time for me to do something for myself."

"I'm glad you did. This was a great class."

"Thank you for coming. And for helping. I see you're new? Unless that's your pink mat," Sylvia said to Rowan.

"Um, no. I'm more of a gray fan. And definitely a yoga virgin."

"Well, I'm happy you decided to end that streak with us. You can tell your friends you lost your virginity with a dozen women at once," Sylvia said.

Rowan snorted a surprised laugh. "I'll have to share that one."

"I hope you'll both come back sometime soon. I'm only hosting a few classes per week right now. I have another teacher starting next week and we'll have a few more classes, but I'm starting slow until I know this will do well."

"Makes sense," Rowan and I both said.

I was a little disappointed that I didn't see anything about the studio opening or about Sylvia hiring, but if I was leaving MacKellar Cove anyway, it didn't matter. I had to find a new path. One that didn't involve living in the same town as my sister.

"I thought so. But I hope this works. And I do hope to see you both back again soon."

"We will. Or, I will," I said.

"I think she can convince me," Rowan said with a wink.

"Well, enjoy the rest of your night. Thanks for coming out."

We waved and said good night and headed out into the cold.

"That was more fun than I thought it would be," Rowan said.

"Really?"

He shrugged. "I like watching you bend and twist in those tight pants. And I like having your hands all over me."

"Again, do you think about anything other than sex?"

"Nope. That's the most important thing."

"Sex is the most important thing? I guess if I was thin I could think that. For me, food is the most important thing."

"Food is up there, but I'd give up food for sex any day. Especially sex like we had."

My cheeks burned at the heated look he raked down my entire body. He stepped closer until I had to tip my head back to look up at him.

"As for you being thin, you don't need to change a thing about yourself."

A ragged laugh tore from my throat. "I think you're the only person in town who feels that way."

The side of his mouth quirked up. "I don't mind being different."

I chewed on my lip and nodded. I didn't mind being different either, most of the time. I didn't know a lot of people who were content to go against the grain, though. Most people wanted to fit in and be invisible in a crowd.

"So, my place or yours?" he asked.

I drew back in shock. "What?"

He raised an eyebrow. "I thought we were going to get food. You said it's the most important thing."

I chuckled. "That is not what you meant."

He grinned. God, it was a beautiful thing. For a man who was more badass than anything else, seeing him smile was stunning. It made me want to see it again.

"Well, if we're already close to a bed…"

He let his words trail off, and I couldn't deny I wanted him again. There was no way for me to resist him. I wanted to tell myself I was starved for attention and affection, and I was, but I genuinely liked him. He was kind and sweet and he was on my side. Or at least, he wasn't on Ramsey's side. It was refreshing.

"I'm not far from here."

"I'll follow you." He grabbed a helmet off the motorcycle parked next to me and snapped it on.

"That's yours?" I asked.

He nodded.

"Isn't it cold?"

He shrugged. "It's the only thing I have."

"Do you want to ride with me?"

He shook his head. "I need to get it back anyway. I'll be fine. You can warm me up when we get to your place."

I bit my lip and hoped he wasn't a popsicle by the time we made it to my place. He climbed on the bike like it was no big deal. The engine roared to life, and my body trembled. If he was still around when it wasn't below freezing, I was going to need to talk him into giving me a ride.

I got in my car and started up the heat to ward off the cold. I glanced over at him, and he gave me a thumb's up, so I pulled out.

I watched him in my mirror on the drive, making sure he was still following me. I pulled into my parking space in the driveway, and he parked right behind me. He got off the bike and removed his helmet, then followed me up to my apartment without a word.

"Fucking hell, it's cold out there," he said when we made it inside. He flexed his fingers and rubbed his hands together.

"Are you okay?"

He nodded. "Especially once I have the most important thing."

"Food?" I asked innocently.

He chuckled. "You might be the death of me."

I grinned and grabbed my takeout menus. "What are you in the mood for?"

His heated gaze raked up and down my body until I was panting and ready to forget all about food and just have him for dinner. He took a step closer and I froze, waiting for him to kiss me or touch me or something.

Then he took the menus from my hand.

I nearly sank to the ground with…I don't know what. It wasn't relief, but it wasn't disappointment either. There was very little doubt we'd end up in my bed later, but he wasn't racing there. He was taking it slow tonight. It was unnerving.

"How about Mediterranean? This sounds good."

I nodded and took the other menus back while he picked something for dinner. When he'd decided, I called in our orders for delivery.

"So, yoga? That's what turns you on. I admit, before

today, I didn't see the appeal," he said when I hung up the phone.

"What?"

"When you told me about the place you said it made you horny even though there was nothing sexual about it. I'm definitely going to argue about that last part, but I kind of get it now."

I shook my head and chuckled. "I really like yoga. I've been doing it for a while and I find it's the only thing that makes me feel good lately."

Rowan went to my couch and took a seat. He crossed one socked foot over the opposite knee and looked at me. "The only thing?"

My cheeks heated and I grinned. "Not the only thing, but one of the only things."

"Ah. I was getting worried there." He grinned at me, then dropped his gaze to his lap. "I understand that, though."

"You do? You seem like a pretty easygoing person."

He shrugged. "I'm trying to be, but it's not always easy. Especially when no one really knows me."

I snorted. "Trust me, I understand that. My sister was my best friend for my whole life, but now…"

"What happened?" he asked.

I looked at him and wondered for the hundredth time if he was just trying to get information. "I'm sure you already know."

He shrugged. "Maybe I'd like to hear your version of it."

"Why?"

"Because people always tell a story from their own point of view. But there are always more sides to a story than just one. I learned that the hard way."

I licked my lips and lowered my gaze. I didn't like him looking at me while I admitted my biggest regret and failure. And it was. What happened with my sister ruined my life, and I regretted it from the moment it happened. But I also couldn't change it.

"I was only about ten when Melody first mentioned Ramsey. She told me about this boy at school and made him sound amazing. I didn't really understand relationships, but when they started dating and Ramsey started coming to our house, I started to get it. He would talk to me and ask me how my day was. My childish brain said he liked me. I was chubby as a kid, not like the girls I grew up with, and not like my sister, so having an attractive, older guy interested in me was intoxicating.

"Over the years, Ramsey and I talked. He told me things about his life that he didn't tell Melody, things about school. I was the first one to know he was going to law school. I thought it meant something. When I was a junior, he came over to our house for New Year's Eve. We were talking and I kissed him. He didn't pull back right away, but he did after a second. I told him I loved him and that we were meant to be together. He proposed to my sister that night."

Rowan sucked in a breath but didn't say anything.

"I was hurt and rejected, but I convinced myself he only married her because I was too young. I know now that it was stupid, but I think a part of me told myself I loved him because he was safe. As long as I believed we were supposed to be together, I didn't have to worry about getting hurt. I didn't have to put myself out there or try to find someone else. I loved him, and if I loved him, of course none of my other relationships were going to work."

Rowan put his hand on my knee and squeezed.

"I didn't try to break them up. I wanted my sister to be happy. Yes, in my twisted head, I wanted Ramsey for myself, but I wanted Melody to be happy, too. Maybe a part of me tried to sabotage their relationship, but I...I don't know. For the last year I've been trying to make sense of it all in my head. I feel like I was another person sometimes. Like I made up stories to make myself believe things. I saw things that weren't there. And I hurt my sister and almost ruined her family because I was jealous of what she had but too afraid to get it for myself."

"So, do you love him?"

I opened my mouth to answer and was interrupted by a knock on the door. Saved by the bell.

10

*R*owan insisted on paying for our dinner. I carried the bag of food to the table and unpacked it while he went in search for drinks. When he sat down again, he said, "You never answered my question."

I sucked in a breath and finally met his gaze. "I don't think I ever loved Ramsey. I loved the idea of him. Of having someone in my life who would look at me the way he did. Not that it was sexual, but like I mattered. He treated me like I was important instead of like I was useless and needed to be tossed aside. And he was good to Melody and Amber. He was that guy I put on a pedestal and measured everyone else against, but I don't think I ever loved him. Not the way she does."

Rowan nodded and opened his container of food. He was silent a few minutes while he ate. I wasn't sure if it was a good sign or a bad one, so I tried to pretend it was okay. I'd gotten good at pretending over the years.

After a few minutes of silence, Rowan said, "My former partner killed himself."

"What?" I breathed.

"It's why I'm here. He got involved with some people who were happy to take down anyone who got in their way. It started as messing up something on their cases so they would get thrown out of court. Then he progressed to concealing evidence that would convict them. By the end, he was doing everything they asked, including building a case against me to take the fall for everything he did."

"Wow."

Rowan nodded. "His conscience got the better of him, and he told me what he did. When I realized what was going on, what he was admitting to, I recorded the conversation as evidence, but the fake documentation was already sent out. My captain tried to tell me for months that something was going on with my partner, but I didn't see it. I didn't want to see it. When the information landed on his desk, he finally put it all together."

"What happened?"

"My partner, John Sanders, had a crisis of conscience and admitted it to me. He told me he was sorry. He asked me to forgive him and to tell his ex-wife and son he was sorry for what he did to them. I was outside his door when the gunshot went off. I broke the door down, but it was too late. He was already gone."

"Oh, my God."

Rowan nodded. "Since the only confession was recorded by me, they didn't trust it. Sanders was dead, so they couldn't ask him. And, of course, the men he worked for weren't really cooperative. I'm here because there's an investigation into the last three years of my career. Technically, I'm on leave. I'm not getting paid for the work I do here. I'm volunteering, but no one knows that except Captain Reynolds. He knows my captain and agreed to let me help out until things get cleared up."

"And then you're going back?" I asked.

He shrugged and nodded. "As long as they clear me, yeah. That was the plan."

I breathed a laugh. "That's why your screen name is Just-Visiting."

He grinned. "I figured it's accurate."

I sucked in a breath at his admission. It shouldn't hurt because I wasn't looking for something long term either. I wanted to leave. Staying in MacKellar Cove was too painful. Why would I want him to stick around if I was leaving?

We weren't a couple. Whatever happened with us was temporary. And I couldn't get upset about it.

"I don't know what's going to happen. If they decide I was the one working for this group, I'm going to jail. If they let me off, they still might not let me have my old job back. There's a lot up in the air right now."

"But you want to go back," I said. It wasn't a question.

He opened his mouth, then shrugged. "I don't know. I did. When I got here, I was pissed off that I was here. That I wasn't allowed to stay put, to do the job I was hired to do. To bring down the people who put Sanders in the position he was in where he thought there was no other choice. I'm trying to take a beat and figure out my life. I'm thirty-three. I have a lot of years left on the force. And I need to make sure I'm on the right one and doing the right things."

"And you don't know where that is anymore."

He shook his head. "I don't. I thought I did, but..." His gaze locked on mine. He sucked in a breath and reached for my hand.

I let him hold it. We were both wounded, both betrayed by people close to us, people we thought we could trust. I thought I could say anything to my sister and she would understand me and get over it, but she didn't. She turned her back on me. And Rowan...his partner was going to let him take the fall for years of illegal activity.

I shook my head. Was I Rowan or was I the partner? Was I the one who was betrayed or was I the one who betrayed someone?

The questions raced through my head and I couldn't answer them. For a year, I told myself Melody was to blame. That she should have given me a chance to explain and talked to me about it, but sitting there with Rowan, I wasn't sure. I was feeling badly for him because his partner lied to him for years, but I did the same thing to my sister.

I had to find a way to apologize to her and make her see that I knew I was wrong. I couldn't go on without her. I didn't want to. I had a lot to make up for, and I had to find a way to do it.

"I need to apologize to my sister," I blurted.

Rowan squeezed my hand. "Now?"

I chuckled. "No. I need to think about what I want to say to her. But she deserves an apology. She needs to know I'm not that person anymore."

"Do you think she'll forgive you?"

I hesitated and shook my head. "I don't think it's about that. I think it's about me needing to own up to my mistakes."

"You know what?"

"What?"

"I think I understand what you meant about yoga. About something that's not sexual at all turning you on."

"Seriously?"

He nodded. "Yeah, because right now, you wanting to talk to your sister is turning me on."

"Really?"

He nodded again. "You're a good person, Willow. I'm glad I wrote you that ticket."

I scoffed. "I'm not. That cost me a hundred bucks."

He grinned. "I think it was worth it."

I raised an eyebrow at him.

His gaze slid down my body and back up again. He moved into my space and in one motion slid one hand to my neck and the other around my back. Before I could think, his lips were on mine, prying my mouth open.

My brain took a few seconds to catch up. When it did, I reached up for him. His skin was warm and heating me up in a hurry. He held me close to him, our bodies connected from our lips to our hips as he pressed me back against the couch. He grew against my stomach and was not shy about showing me how much he wanted me.

He stood and pulled me up with him. His hands dipped to my hips and he guided me to the bedroom. I didn't even try to resist him. I didn't want to. I wanted him. All of him.

He pulled back when we made it to the side of the bed. He was breathing as hard as I was, both of us struggling to keep it together. "Take off your clothes," he commanded me.

I tilted my head. "I thought you said I could be in charge."

He smirked. "Fine. After you get naked, you can be in charge."

I raised an eyebrow at him. "Take off your clothes, too."

He grinned. "With pleasure."

He let his zip-up slide off his shoulders and fall on the floor behind him. Then he grabbed his shirt with one hand and stripped it off, tossing it on top of his sweatshirt. His hands stilled at the waist of his sweatpants and he looked up at me expectantly.

"You just like watching me strip, don't you?"

I raised an eyebrow. "A blind woman would enjoy this show."

He chuckled. "Why don't you close your eyes then?"

My breath hitched at the rough tone of his voice. Commanding and teasing at once. I let my eyes fall closed.

And waited.

I didn't know what he was going to do, but as I stood

there with my eyes closed, listening for him to move, every cell in my body stilled.

His hand touched my neck, and I jumped. My eyes flew open.

"Relax, Willow."

I closed my eyes again and drew in a deep breath. I tensed when his hand brushed my hair to the side, but I kept my eyes closed. He kissed the part of my neck he exposed, then licked his way to the collar of my shirt. One arm eased around my waist and pulled me flush to him.

"I like having you against me."

"Me, too," I whispered.

"I like touching you," he said. His hand lifted my shirt slightly, then slid into my pants. He kept going, his fingers teasing my sensitive flesh until he met my wet center.

I moaned softly and leaned back, spreading my thighs.

"I like the way you respond to me. How you give yourself over to me and let me touch you."

I nodded. His other hand found mine and wound our fingers together. He brought our hands up to my breast and teased my pert nipple through the layers of fabric I still wore.

"Are you going to come for me, Willow? Just like this? With your eyes closed, letting me touch you?"

"Yes," I whispered.

"I can't wait to be inside you. Having your hands on me all class was torture. I wanted to just say fuck it, and have you right then. But I'm really happy these pants are so stretchy so I can watch you bend and twist in them, then slide my hand inside and fuck you with my fingers."

I moaned loudly, and his cock twitched against my back. His fingers speared into me, stealing all the thoughts from my head. My body wanted him. Needed him. He pressed his thumb to my clit, and I couldn't hold back.

I bucked against his hand and called out his name. I never

thought of yoga as foreplay, but I'd never done yoga with Rowan before. Watching him and touching him had turned me on as much as it did him, and I was wet and ready for him before his first touch.

He didn't let me stop at one and toyed with my body as I rode out my orgasm.

"You're so fucking gorgeous when you come. Again, Willow. Again."

He rubbed his thumb over my clit and my body responded to him. I was at the edge and falling when he nipped my shoulder and said, "Open your eyes. Watch as you come for me."

My eyes flipped open and I saw the two of us in my mirror. His hand disappeared into my pants, the bulge in the front moving as he stroked my clit. Our joined hands cupped my breasts, his fingers teasing my nipple. And behind me, he was completely naked. His body rocked with mine, riding out my orgasm with me.

And then I saw his eyes. Dark eyes blazing into mine in the mirror. Watching me, taking in everything. Staring at him, I lost all control. My orgasm shook through me, but I refused to break eye contact with him. He stared at my reflection as I stared at his. I moaned and screamed and rode his hand without a care in the world.

"Fucking beautiful," he whispered against my neck. "I need you, Willow. Right now."

He yanked my pants down, both of us struggling to get me free. When his hand was available, he grabbed a condom and rolled it on. I was bent at the waist, trying to pull my pants off, when he stepped up behind me and grabbed my hips.

His cock slid over my flesh. I spread my thighs and grabbed the edge of my bed. When I pushed back against him, he groaned.

Then he slammed into me with one hard stroke.

"Oh, God," I moaned.

"Jesus, I'm not gonna last long," he groaned.

His fingers bit into my hips. The pain grounded me, centering me. I looked up at the mirror and found him watching me. I crossed my arms on the edge of the bed and looked at him. His jaw was clenched tight, his muscles corded and tense. His eyes were darker than black. Everything about him said determined and focused, but every so often, he glanced down. Breaking our eye contact.

I pushed back against him, feeling the pull of another orgasm. He tilted his hips and found the spot that was just out of reach. I gasped, instantly closer. He did it again, and I was right there. Just that quickly, he brought me to the edge.

"Willow," he groaned.

The one word, just my name, was a plea, a request, a demand, all at once. I answered it on his next stroke, my body letting go. I squeezed around him, not letting him out, and he responded with the same need. He slammed into me once more, and stilled, holding himself deep inside me as our bodies pulsed.

We stayed like that, locked together and staring at each other, until our bodies cooled. Only then did Rowan move. His eyes stayed on mine as he slid out. He kissed my shoulder and ran a hand up my spine.

"I'll be right back," he whispered.

I nodded, unsure what I was supposed to do. The other times, he was one and done, disappearing into the night like a thief with something to hide. I wasn't expecting him to stay.

But I also wasn't opposed to it.

When he walked out of the bathroom, I was sitting on the edge of the bed, still trying to decide what I should do. The edge of his mouth quirked up.

He moved toward me like he owned me. Like he controlled everything about me. And with his gaze pinned on me and my body still warm from sex, I couldn't deny that maybe he did.

94

11

After stalking Balanced Life online the following weekend, I saw there was a late morning class on Wednesday. Since I was off, I headed over there to check it out, hoping to make it a regular thing. At least until I could find something else.

Jobs were scarce unless I wanted to move to a city. Syracuse was a few hours away, but I'd never lived in a city and wasn't really sure about it. There were things I really didn't like about living in MacKellar Cove, but I knew going from a town of a few thousand people to a city was a huge change. One I wasn't willing to make just yet.

The studio was quiet again, but there was a low level of buzz to the quiet. I found a spot in the studio and did my best to calm my mind before class started. Some instructors jumped right in and some gave us a little more time to get centered, but I knew I needed an extra minute before class started to be focused and ready.

I'd just finished my breathing exercises when Sylvia walked over to me. I said hello and asked how she was doing.

"A little stressed right now, to be honest. I hate to do this to you, but I wondered if I could ask you a huge favor. Have you ever taught a class?"

I shook my head. My stomach dropped to the floor. She was going to kick me out? Seriously? I'd already been there.

"Shoot. You were so good that I assumed you were an instructor. I was going to ask if you would be willing to teach this class. I knew it was a long shot, but the woman I hired just called and she…well, she isn't going to work out. I have a private lesson booked in the other studio, and I was hoping I wouldn't have to cancel this class—"

"I'll do it," I blurted.

"You will?"

I nodded. "I will. I don't mind at all. And, um, if you're looking to hire someone else, I'd love to be considered for it."

"Really? I thought you said you've never taught."

"I…I haven't, but I want to. I interviewed at another studio, and…I know I'm a risk and I have no experience and I don't look like a yoga instructor should—"

"I don't know who told you that, but they are wrong. You are a beautiful woman, and you don't need anyone to tell you what you should look like. Let's talk after class. If that's okay with you."

I nodded. "That would be great."

"Thank you so much. I really appreciate the help, Willow."

"I'm happy to do it. I promise, I'll do my best."

"I know you will. That's why I asked you."

Her confidence in me made me feel like I could do anything. She squeezed my arm and waved as she hurried out of the room. I carried my mat to the front of the studio and laid it out. Then I addressed the class.

"Hello, everyone. I'm Willow. I'll be teaching this class today. It's my first class, but I'm hoping not my last. If you have any suggestions for me when we're finished, I'd love to know what you thought. Thank you."

The others in the class smiled and nodded their heads, keeping things quiet and serene. I started class with stretching and breathing exercises that I knew everyone would be able to handle, then I moved on to moves that took a little more strength and flexibility.

I tried to remember what I'd learned from other yoga classes and demonstrated each pose then walked around the class and helped others if they weren't in the correct position. I showed everyone poses for beginner, intermediate, and advanced students, doing my best to keep the class at a level where everyone was comfortable.

I was surprised when I looked at the clock and the class was almost over. I led them through a short cool down and stretches and thanked them all for being there.

I taught my first yoga class. It felt great.

"Thank you for teaching today," one lady said when she approached me. "This was my first yoga class ever, and I was nervous, but you made me feel very comfortable. I never would have known you were new to teaching. You were wonderful."

"Thank you," I told her, beaming with her praise.

The rest of the students who approached shared similar thoughts and by the time the studio was empty, I was floating. I could feel everything inside me lining up. This was what I was meant to do.

Sylvia walked in while I was rolling up my mat. "You were a hit," she said.

"Thank you. I think they were wonderful. And this was… amazing. Thank you for asking me."

"I need to be thanking you. If you hadn't said yes, I would have had to cancel this class. I owe you. And judging by the conversation on the way out and the things I overheard, I need to hire you."

"Are you serious?"

Sylvia nodded. "I am. I wanted to have a second person working here with me. Like I said, the other woman isn't going to work out, but I'd like you to consider it. If you were serious. Maybe we start with a month long trial basis so we can learn if we work well together. And if things go well, then we can talk about setting up some classes that you teach on your own."

My smile was so big I thought my cheeks were going to split. But before I could say yes, I hesitated.

"I really appreciate this. I can't tell you how much. Honestly, I've been considering leaving the area. It's been a rough year for me, and I've been thinking about going some-where else."

"Oh," Sylvia said. "Well, I'm sorry to hear that."

I nodded. "Can I think about it? Because I really enjoyed this class, and I've been undecided lately about where I want to be. I just don't want to leave you in the same position you're in now."

"Thank you for your honesty. Not everyone would tell the truth, but I really appreciate it. How about this? Over the next month, we'll work together on classes. You can take some of them and I'll take some of them. I'll make sure I'm available for all the classes, just in case. I won't double book anything. If at the end of the month, we're both happy with the arrangement, we come up with a new plan. If by then, you decide you are serious about leaving, we'll go from there. Does that work?"

Shocked wasn't even close to how I felt. She wanted to give me a chance, even though I told her I might be leaving. "That sounds amazing. Are you sure?"

Sylvia nodded. "I am. I know you're good at this, and I want someone to work with me who has a passion for yoga like I do. I see that in you, but I also understand needing to follow your own path. Give it some thought and see how you feel, and we'll go from there."

"Thank you, Sylvia. I…thank you."

We talked a few more minutes and she asked my availability for the classes the rest of the week. We came up with a plan and I walked out the door with a new job.

That was definitely not what I expected. But it was amazing.

I was still flying high when I got back into town. I was starving and wanted to celebrate, so I went to Just Tacos. I didn't care that I was alone, I just wanted a chicken taco and a margarita for lunch.

I smiled at the hostess and followed her to a table for one. I thanked her and took the menu even though I knew what I was getting. I flipped through in case something else jumped out at me and decided to splurge on queso and chips, too.

The server came over and took my order, then left me alone at the table again. I couldn't stop smiling and was starting to worry I looked like a crazy person. I pulled out my phone so at least I could pretend I was smiling at something on there.

The server delivered my margarita and said my lunch would be out soon. I opened the Book Boyfriends Wanted app and pulled up my conversations with Rowan. One day I needed to get his phone number. Maybe. If we both stayed in MacKellar Cove. For the moment, having him only on the app made it safer. If we ended, I could delete him from my matches instead of having to delete his contact from my phone.

I sent him a message asking how his day was and waited for his reply.

JUSTVISITING

Boring.

UPFORANYTHING

I guess that's good for a cop.

JUSTVISITING

Sometimes. It's more interesting when something happens during the day. Doesn't have to be much.

UPFORANYTHING

You're wishing for someone to commit a crime. I think there might be something wrong with you.

JUSTVISITING

Probably true. How's your day?

UPFORANYTHING

Great actually. I went back to the yoga studio and taught a class.

JUSTVISITING

Dammit. Now I'm horny. Why did you tell me that? And why didn't you take me with you? I would have paid good money to see you demonstrating all those poses.

I laughed and shook my head at him.

UPFORANYTHING

I'm teaching again. Maybe you can take another class with me.

JUSTVISITING

I'll quit my job if I have to. I'll be there.

I laughed and set my phone down when the server delivered my lunch. "Anything else?" he asked.

I shook my head. "This looks great. Thank you."

He nodded and walked away, leaving me to my food. And Rowan.

UPFORANYTHING

I'll send you my schedule. For now, I'm eating lunch. My taco is waiting for me.

JUSTVISITING

I could go for a taco. Where are you? Order me a water and four chicken tacos.

I pulled back, surprised he wanted to join me.

JUSTVISITING

Sorry. I should have said do you mind if I join you?

I laughed.

UPFORANYTHING

No, I don't mind. Sounds good to me. I'll put in your order. I'm at Just Tacos.

JUSTVISITING

On my way.

I caught the server's attention and asked him to add Rowan's order to mine. He nodded and wrote it down before he walked away.

I glanced at the door, watching for Rowan to appear, and my breath hitched. Melody and Amber were sitting at a table on the other side of the restaurant. No, they were getting up from a table on the other side of the restaurant. And had to walk past my table in order to leave.

My heart pounded in my ears. My breath rushed out of me. I watched them until they disappeared behind the booths that separated us. I told myself to let them walk by me, but I didn't want to. I wanted to talk to my sister.

"Hi, Melody," I said when they were next to my table.

She turned with a bright smile on her face. Her gaze

landed on mine and the smile melted away. Icy disdain filled her eyes. Her lips pinched together in pain.

"Willow."

"How are you?" I asked her. "Hi, Amber."

"Hi, Aunt Willow. Why don't you come see me anymore?"

I glanced up at Melody, but she was looking at her daughter. "Aunt Willow and Mommy had a fight."

"You always tell me I have to forgive my friends when we fight. Why shouldn't you forgive Aunt Willow?" Amber asked.

"Some things are unforgivable," Melody said.

The coldness in her voice was unmistakable. She had no interest in anything I had to say. But I had to try.

"I'm sorry, Melody. I am. More than you could know. I wish—"

"That you'd never kissed my husband or that I never found out about it? Oh, no wait, you wish I'd listened to your lies and left him so you could have him. Is that the one?"

"No," I said softly.

"I don't know what you thought I would say, Willow. Did you really think you could apologize and I would forgive you?"

"We've always forgiven each other. For everything."

"And you've never done anything like this before. I trusted you. I thought you were on my side. I thought you were my best friend. I shared things with you I never told another person, even Ramsey. And you used it all against me so you could ruin my marriage. So you could have my husband for yourself."

"I didn't—"

"Hello, ladies," Rowan said, appearing behind Melody like a beacon of hope. "How is everyone today?"

Melody turned and looked up at him. "Hi, Rowan. I'm sorry. I wasn't trying to cause a problem."

I should have known they were friends. They probably all got together on a regular basis or something. And as usual, I was on the outside.

"Good. Is everything okay?" Rowan asked.

Melody shook her head. "Not really. But I'm leaving. I'm sorry we created an issue. I wish they'd said something to us instead of calling you."

"No one called me. I'm here for lunch."

Of course, the server chose that moment to walk over and set Rowan's plate down on my table.

Rowan looked up at me and smiled. "Looks great. Thanks for ordering for me."

"You're having lunch together?" Melody asked.

Rowan nodded. "Yep. I'd ask if you want to join us, but it looks like you've already finished." He pointed to the to-go box Amber carried.

Melody's gaze flipped between us like she couldn't figure out what was happening. "You're...are you...what...?"

"It was good to see you, Melody. Say hi to Ramsey," Rowan said as he moved around them and took the seat opposite me.

I watched as my sister figured out what was going on. Her gaze flickered to mine, and she gave me a hard glare. I didn't know why it was an issue that I was seeing Rowan, but obviously it was.

Melody guided Amber toward the door without another word. I watched them get in her minivan and leave, absorbing everything I could about them before they vanished from my sight.

"Are you okay?" Rowan asked after a minute.

I forced a smile and nodded. "Yeah, I'm great."

"You're also full of shit. What was that about?"

"I didn't know you two were friends."

He shook his head and swallowed a bite of his taco.

"We're not. Not really. I know Ramsey, and I've met Melody a few times."

"You acted like you didn't know who they were."

He nodded while he chewed another bite. "I told you I wanted to hear things from you, not someone else. There are always two sides to a story."

"And one side is always wrong."

He shook his head. "I didn't say that, Willow. I'm not here right now because of Melody. I'm here for—"

"Tacos," I said.

He chuckled. "That, too."

I tried to grin. I had no right to get upset with him. It bothered me that he was friendly with Melody, but I wasn't surprised by it. I just had to wrap my head around the idea and know that she was probably going to talk him into ending things.

Like everyone else in town. No big surprise there, except Melody was the one person who could probably actually do it.

And that scared me.

12

ROWAN

Willow was quiet through most of the rest of lunch. I tried to ask her questions and get her talking, but she was distracted. It wasn't a surprise, but it bothered me. She was pushed out of so many things and the whole town had turned against her. All because of a crush on a boy who was nice to her when no other boy paid her any attention.

Maybe I was missing something to the story, but I couldn't see where Willow was the only bad guy. I found myself laying more blame at Ramsey's feet than Willow's. He didn't mean to lead her on, but he also was the adult in the situation. It didn't excuse what happened after she kissed him, but I couldn't stop wondering what happened during the years in between.

I paid for our lunches and walked outside with Willow, following her to her car. My SUV was next to hers, but I went to the driver's door with her so I could have another minute.

"If I don't hear from you again, I understand," she said

softly. Her lips curled up in a sad, forced smile. She avoided looking at me.

I tilted her chin up and waited until she met my gaze. A tear slid free and ran down her cheek, soaking into my thumb. She closed her eyes again, hiding her feelings from me.

It broke me to see her in so much pain. To know one conversation with her sister could upset her so much. She was strong and fierce, but she didn't want me to see how much everything hurt.

I leaned closer until her breath became mine. Her eyes asked the question, and my body answered, pressing against her as I claimed her lips.

And she claimed my heart.

I didn't know where in the hell that came from, but the moment our lips touched I knew she was it for me. We were having fun. The sex was amazing and spending time with her was supposed to be a distraction.

But somewhere along the way, I fell for her. Hard. So hard that I wanted to shield her from everyone who even thought about hurting her. From anyone who threatened her.

I pulled back just enough that I could see her face. I scanned it, taking in every freckle and wrinkle while she breathed deeply. She was waiting for me to end things, but she was going to have to wait a long time because I wasn't going anywhere.

"Thank you for coming to my rescue," she said softly.

"Any time. Although next time, instead of tacos I demand a yoga class as my payment."

"You didn't even let me pay for the tacos," she said with a laugh, finally looking like the woman I loved.

The words rolled around in my head while she laughed. *The woman I loved.* I'd never thought those words before.

There were women who said they loved me, women I wanted to love, but never women I loved. Not until Willow.

"Let me know when you're teaching again," I told her, ignoring her comment about paying. She wasn't going to worry about anything if I could help it. She'd had too much happen in the last year. She deserved to be taken care of for once instead of having to do everything on her own.

"I will," she said with a nod. "You should probably get back to work."

"To my endlessly boring day?"

She chuckled.

"I suppose. Can I see you tonight?"

She looked up at me then nodded, drawing her lips between her teeth.

"Good. I'll bring dinner."

"Dinner? Lunch and dinner on the same day?"

I nuzzled her neck. "I'm hoping I can talk you into breakfast in the morning, too."

She moaned softly and ran her hands through my hair. "You're going to spoil me. Then when you leave, I'm not going to know what to do with myself."

Leaving. I forgot about that. I pulled back quickly, the reality of my world hitting me between the shoulder blades. "We don't have to worry about that yet."

She nodded slowly. The walls between us went back up. Mine, not hers. Maybe some of hers, too. We were both protecting ourselves.

"I'll see you tonight," I said. I gave her another quick kiss then walked around the front of my vehicle and got in. I waited until she backed out of her spot and left before I did the same, turning the opposite direction and going back to work.

When I walked back into the precinct, one of the young

cops who was only with us part time said, "Hey, Captain Reynolds was looking for you."

"I was out to lunch," I told him.

"He wasn't pissed. Just asked if anyone had seen you."

"Thanks."

The Captain's door was closed so I knocked and waited for him to tell me I could come in.

"Masterson, good. I need to talk to you. Close the door," Captain Reynolds said.

I closed the door and drew a breath. It was rarely good when he called me into his office. And after the lunch I had with Willow, I almost expected him to tell me I should stop seeing her.

"What can I do for you, sir?"

"Relax, Masterson. I got a call from Captain Bray."

My heart kicked into overdrive and my palms instantly dampened. I was torn between wanting to make a run for it and wanting to throw up. All I knew was in that room was the last place I wanted to be. Captain Bray was my captain in Phoenix and a call from him meant an update.

"Take a breath, Masterson. It's all good news."

My hands shook but I nodded. Even good news wasn't good news. Good news meant…I didn't know what it meant.

"They cleared you of everything. Bray said your former partner laid everything out in a document they found on his personal computer. He kept records of everything he did. It sounds like it was only in the last year or so, but it was enough for them to determine you weren't involved."

I took a breath and nodded. "Thank you, sir."

"This is good news, Masterson. Why do you look like I just told you someone is outside the door with cuffs for you?"

"It's just a shock, sir. I wasn't expecting to hear anything for a while. And I just…it's good news."

"You fell in love, didn't you?" Reynolds said with a laugh. He leaned back in his chair and grinned.

"Excuse me?" How the fuck did he know that?

"MacKellar Cove sneaks up on people and grabs a hold of you. I get it."

"Yes, sir," I told him. I could run with that excuse.

"Let me take a look at my budget, Masterson. You've been an asset to us, and I'd hate to lose you if you have an interest in sticking around."

I nodded. "Thank you, sir."

"I can't make any promises, but I'll see what I can do. But you need to call Bray. You need to get the report from him."

"I will. Thank you, sir."

He turned back to his computer and I took the hint and left. I walked back to my desk woodenly, trying to wrap my head around the day.

Going back to Phoenix meant returning to my life. My old squad. Righting the wrongs done there. It also meant leaving Willow.

But staying? Could I give up everything for Willow? And that meant Reynolds finding a job for me.

I pushed the decision aside and went out to my MacKellar Cove SUV to call Bray. He was thrilled about the decision and ready for me to get back to work ASAP.

"If you have any cases you're finishing up, I understand needing to stick around and close things," Bray said.

"Thanks."

"I don't know how you handled being there this long. I was pushing to get this all wrapped up so you could come back to civilization. I bet you're going out of your mind." Bray chuckled.

"Something like that," I told him.

"Listen, I know you're worried about the guys here. I've been talking to them and telling everyone what happened. As much as I can. There are going to be some that give you shit, but for the most part, everything will be right back to normal. I don't know who your new partner is going to be, but it'll be fine. Everything will be fine," Bray said.

I nodded and drew in a breath. I didn't know how to tell him I wasn't sure if I wanted to come back at all. Lucky for me, he kept talking and I didn't have to say a thing.

"Hey, I gotta run. You know how things are. But it's good to talk to you. We'll be in touch soon."

"Sounds good," I said.

He hung up, already yelling at someone else before the phone turned off. For months, I missed the fast pace and the closure of solving a case and putting away the bad guys. But just like Willow, somewhere along the way, things changed. I changed.

Captain Reynolds was right. I was starting to think of MacKellar Cove as home. As the place I wanted to be. And leaving was a hard pill to swallow.

One I wasn't sure I could.

I GOT to Willow's later than I planned that evening. I got caught up at work since I was distracted all afternoon and needed to stay late to finish up paperwork from the day. I expected her to be mad at me.

"Um, hi," she said when she answered the door. Her hair was piled on top of her head in a knot thing. She wore a hoodie that was about three sizes too big and leggings that hugged her thighs and made me hard.

"Hey," I said. "Did you forget I was coming over?"

She shook her head and stepped back to let me in. "I just figured you weren't coming when you didn't show up earlier."

"I had to work late. I should have reached out."

"It's fine," she said.

Kiss of death. Nothing was ever fine with a woman. "I'm sorry, okay. I didn't realize how late it was. We didn't really set a time, so I had no idea there was a limit on when I could show up."

She crossed her arms and stared up at me. The woman I'd fallen for wasn't there. The woman looking back at me was beaten and bruised, defeated. She wanted to throw me out and tell me to go to hell, but she was too tired.

Her lips trembled for just a moment, then she clamped it between her teeth. She sucked in a breath and nodded. Dammit.

"I'm sorry, Willow. I'm on edge and taking it out on you. I shouldn't have said that."

"It's fine. You didn't have to come. Maybe you should just leave."

"I don't want to leave," I told her, moving closer to her. She didn't back away, but she didn't sink into me when I wrapped my arms around her and hugged her close. She stood still, stiff, uncomfortable with me.

I didn't want to let her go, but I did anyway. I took a step back and looked at her. She closed her eyes and licked her lips.

"What happened?"

She shook her head. "Nothing."

"I don't believe you."

She shrugged. "It doesn't matter if you believe me or not. You're leaving soon."

"Did Captain Reynolds tell you? He shouldn't have said anything about that. It's not his news to share."

She shook her head and leveled me with a glare. "I haven't spoken to him. But obviously something happened today. Is that really why you're late?"

I sighed and ran a hand through my hair. I wanted to tell her everything. From falling for her to wanting to stay, but she was a runner. She didn't know how to let me in. If I pushed too far too fast, she was going to disappear.

"My former captain called. I've been cleared of all charges."

She forced a smile. "That's great news. Congratulations."

I nodded. "Thanks."

"When are you leaving?"

"I don't know yet."

She nodded again. "Well, this is what you wanted. What you've been waiting for. It's really great. I hope you're happy."

"Willow…"

"We should celebrate. Eat dinner. I think I have some beer in the fridge," she said. She moved around me to the kitchen, avoiding touching me.

I wanted to reach out to her, but she was too far away. I needed her to ground me, to tell me what the best thing was, but she already wrote me off and had me leaving.

She grabbed two beer bottles and carried them to the couch. She started unpacking the food I brought over and resumed the show she was watching. I sat with her and tried to pretend nothing strange was going on.

We barely talked while we ate. She laughed at the show and acted like I wasn't even there. When the show was over and the food was gone, she cleaned up and curled back into herself on the far side of the couch.

"I don't want to leave," I admitted quietly.

"What?"

"I don't want to leave. I really like it here." I looked at her, hoping she understood what I wasn't saying.

She sucked in a breath and stared back at me. She understood. "You do?"

I nodded. "Yeah, I do. Especially if you start teaching yoga in the area and you stick around."

She nodded slowly and finally moved closer to me. She rested her head on my shoulder and said, "I would really like that."

I kissed the top of her head and slid my arm around her. This was where I was supposed to be. With Willow in the tiny town I'd never heard of before I was exiled there. With people who wormed their way into me and made this place home.

"Is there a job available for you?" Willow asked.

"Captain Reynolds is going to see what he can do."

Willow nodded against my chest. "Well, until we know for sure, we need to make every moment we have together count."

"Oh, yeah? And how do you plan to do that?" I asked.

She sat up and grinned, then crawled on my lap and kissed the hell out of me. Great minds definitely were thinking alike on that one.

13

O'Kelley's was relatively quiet when I walked in Thursday night. The guys were already at the bar, talking and laughing at something Gavin said. I headed straight there, taking a seat on the end next to Ramsey.

Hudson set a beer down in front of me. I nodded at him in thanks and brought it to my lips as I listened to the conversation already in progress.

"Having my girlfriend work for you is trouble," Gavin grumbled.

"Having my wife work here was no fun either," Ramsey said.

"Melody worked here?" I asked.

Ramsey nodded. "For a few months when we were apart last year. She was starting up her business and wanted to have consistent income since we were separated. She only worked here during the day, but I hated every second of it."

"I loved it," Hudson said. "She kept everything in line. My books haven't been that organized ever."

"Maybe you should hire someone else to handle it," Ian

suggested. "Finley is a master at that stuff and will double check things for me. She's got an incredible head for business."

"Think she'd do it?" Hudson asked.

Ian shrugged. "You can always ask her."

"I never thought I'd be unhappy that you and Melody worked things out," Hudson said with a wry grin for Ramsey.

Ramsey chuckled. "You're not alone." He swung his gaze to me. "I hear you're still seeing Willow. Mel said you met her for lunch the other day."

I nodded. "Yep."

"You're not at all worried about being involved with her?"

I shook my head.

"Be careful. She doesn't care who she hurts when it comes to getting what she wants," Ramsey said.

"And you still think she wants you?" I asked.

He paused with a beer halfway to his lips. He set it down and looked at me. "I hope not. I really do. I liked Willow when she was young, before she kissed me. She was a great person. Funny and kind. After that, everything changed. I hope that person is still inside and that she can be happy."

"Did you ever think maybe it's your fault that she changed?" I asked him.

Ramsey pulled back and glared at me. The others sucked in a breath and froze. I didn't like that Willow was the one who was berated and Ramsey walked around with his head held high like he was untouchable. Why? Why didn't he have to answer for the way he treated her?

"How could I be to blame for Willow?" Ramsey asked.

I shrugged. "Maybe how great you thought she was made it seem like you wanted more from her. Maybe what you thought was being friendly was flirtatious in her mind."

"I didn't intend for it to be."

"Intent only goes so far."

Ramsey sighed. "You're right. Maybe there was a part of me that liked the fact that Willow had me on a pedestal. But that was years ago. Melody and I have been married eleven years. Why did Willow hang onto that for so long? That's not on me. I pulled back after she kissed me. I did everything I could, short of being cruel, to make her understand I was in love with Melody and not her. At some point, Willow has to accept responsibility for her actions and not blame them on me and whatever she thinks I did forever ago."

I wanted to argue with him, but Ramsey was right. Willow was an adult. If she'd tried to break up Melody and Ramsey before they got married, I could almost see it as her being a jealous kid, but it had been years.

Did that mean she was still holding out hope that Ramsey would choose her?

I wasn't entirely sure I wanted that answer.

I DIDN'T RESPOND to Willow's messages after I left O'Kelley's. I was still processing everything Ramsey said. I was trying to make a decision about my future with a woman that I wasn't sure wanted me in hers.

After I checked in at the precinct the next morning, I headed to Cracked for breakfast. I wasn't hungry when I got up, but I was starving by the time I left, and Captain Reynolds never had an issue with us getting something to eat while we were on the clock.

Blake was pouring coffee and talking to the regulars when I walked in. I waved hello to a few people I recognized, still wondering when MacKellar Cove snuck up and grabbed a hold of me. I took a seat at a table alone, hoping I could eat a quick breakfast without having to talk to everyone in the restaurant.

"Coffee?" Blake asked, holding the pot up.

I nodded. "Please."

She filled my mug and asked if I was ready to order.

"Not yet," I said.

"I'll grab the cream and sugar for you and be right back."

I studied the menu while she checked in on other tables. Everything I'd had there was good. It was only a matter of narrowing down the options to decide what I was in the mood for.

The front door opened, but I ignored it in favor of the menu. Whoever it was wasn't there to see me, and I wasn't in a friendly mood, so it didn't matter.

Until she took the seat across from me.

"Hey, Rowan," Melody said.

I looked up. "Melody."

"Can I join you?" she asked.

Blake came over and filled her mug without a word, leaving the cream and sugar on the table for us. She was gone before I could answer Melody.

"I guess you have, so sure." I gave her a less than friendly smile. I liked Melody, but not when she was being nasty to Willow.

Melody picked up a menu from the center of the table and studied it. We ignored each other until Blake took our orders and we put our menus back and had no choice but to look at each other.

"So, to what do I owe the pleasure?" I asked her.

"I know you've been spending time with my sister."

I raised an eyebrow because of course she knew. Not only did everyone in town know everyone else's business, but she saw us together just a few days earlier.

"How is she?"

"Excuse me?"

Melody drew in a shaky breath. "Maybe it's not fair of me to ask you, but I want to know how Willow is. Is she okay?"

"No, it's not fair of you to ask me. Especially after you made her feel like shit the other day."

Melody nodded and dropped her chin. "I know. I wish I hadn't. I'm still…she hurt me." Melody met my gaze with a watery one. A tear streaked down her cheek. She brushed it away quickly but another one followed. "She was my best friend. For my whole life, she was the one person I counted on. Growing up, she was there for me. Being five years apart never mattered that much. She was the person I told every-thing to. And losing her has been really hard."

"You didn't have to lose her," I said.

Melody nodded, her brown hair falling forward over her shoulder. She tucked it behind her ears and forced a smile. "A part of me wishes I'd handled things with Willow differently. That I could have salvaged my relationship with her. But I don't know how. I don't know if it was really possible."

"Why not?" I asked. I needed to know. Melody knew Willow better than anyone else. Her tears proved she still loved her sister. I wanted to know if Willow was the person I thought she was. If she was someone I could take a chance on. If I could risk loving her and have any hope that she felt the same.

"I love my sister. That will never change. But I don't know if I can ever trust her again. She used my desire to have a family against me. She manipulated me into creating prob-lems with my husband. How can I trust her?"

I sighed. Things were getting complicated with Willow. Maybe it was better I just leave. Go back to Phoenix and forget all about her. Because if Melody was right, or if Ramsey was right, and Willow couldn't be trusted, it was because she still wanted Ramsey for herself.

"Can I trust my sister?" Melody asked quietly.

I met her gaze and saw the depth of her desire. She wanted to trust Willow again. She missed her sister. I could see it and feel it. She was as unhappy as Willow was. Which meant maybe they could repair their relationship.

"I don't think I can answer that for you," I told her.

Blake brought our breakfast over and asked if we needed anything else. We said no, and Blake squeezed Melody's shoulder before walking away. Willow told me about their friendship. That Melody only got to know Blake and the rest of the women in that circle around the time she and Willow stopped talking. Melody moved on to other people, gaining a whole new circle of friends, and Willow was left alone, with no one on her side.

"Willow is a good person. She's funny and kind and passionate about so many things. She's the kind of person I think we all want in our lives because she pushes us to be better. She's not perfect, but none of us are. I also don't think she's the only one at fault through all this. She knows she wasn't right trying to break you and Ramsey up, but can you really sit there and tell me that your marriage was perfect? That if it was as strong as you want to believe that your sister could have pushed you to that point?"

"I..." Melody thought about it and shook her head. "You're right. Things with Ramsey were fragile after we lost Steven. I felt like it was my fault. I turned to Willow instead of Ramsey to heal. I told her things about our marriage that I never should have told anyone. She exploited that, though."

"She's not blameless," I admitted. "But none of you are. I'm not going to defend her or try to blame you, but it's easy for her to be the bad one. She's the only one who's been punished for what happened. For admitting the truth."

"Do you think she still wants Ramsey?" Melody asked softly.

I looked at her and tried to smile. "I hope not."

Melody smiled back and reached across the table. She put her hand on my arm and said, "Me, too."

WHEN I FINISHED my shift that night, I sent Willow a message on the app. I really needed to get her phone number.

JUSTVISITING

Want to come over for dinner?

UPFORANYTHING

Nope.

JUSTVISITING

Okay, how about I come to your place?

UPFORANYTHING

Not interested.

JUSTVISITING

Are you okay?

UPFORANYTHING

I'm great.

JUSTVISITING

Then what's going on?

UPFORANYTHING

Why don't you ask my sister. You two were pretty cozy this morning at breakfast.

Fucking hell.

JUSTVISITING

We were talking about you.

UPFORANYTHING

Hope it was fun. I'll save you the trouble of ending things and tell you we're done.

JUSTVISITING

Are you serious?

I waited for her to reply, but she signed out of the app. I yelled and slammed my fist into the steering wheel. The horn blasted, and another cop walking by jumped. I waved to tell him sorry.

I tore out of the parking lot and raced to Willow's apartment. I pounded on the door and waited. It was dark inside, but something told me she was home.

I strained to hear something, anything, that told me she was there, but it was silent inside her apartment. I tried the app again, but she was still not logged in. Dammit.

The last thing I wanted to do was ask Ramsey for her number, but I knew he would have it. I sent him a text and asked him to share her contact info with me.

Why?

Because I need it.

I could almost hear the disapproval in his silence, but a minute later, the contact showed up. I saved it and sent her a text.

And heard the tone inside her apartment.

I sent another text, telling her I knew she was in there and to let me in. And another one saying it was me.

Go away, Rowan.

No. We need to talk.

"Why?" she asked through the closed door.

"Because you owe me at least that much," I said, knowing it would piss her off.

"I owe you?" she shouted back. "I owe you? Are you kidding me?" She yanked the door open to yell at me face-to-face, and I pushed my way inside.

"Yes, you owe me."

"Get out," she said.

"No. You're being a child. We need to talk."

"I don't want to hear it. Melody wants you to end things with me. Ramsey and Hudson and everyone else you know want you to end things. So, just go away, Rowan. Leave me alone."

"I don't want to end things. And that's not why Melody ambushed me at breakfast. She wants to know if you're okay."

"Why?" Willow scoffed.

"Because she cares about you. You hurt her, but she misses you."

"She hurt me, too."

I nodded. "I know she did. And I told her that. She doesn't know if she can trust you. She thinks you still want Ramsey."

Her gaze snapped to mine. "Did you tell her that?"

"I told her I hope you don't."

Willow held my gaze for a minute then turned and walked away. She went to the couch and hugged a pillow to her chest. She looked young and scared for the first time ever. The woman I knew was strong and fierce. She didn't back down from anything.

"You need to fight back," I said. "You need to face Melody and Ramsey. They need to know you're not the only one to blame for all this. You're not the teenager you were when you kissed Ramsey. You need to accept that you messed up last year and take control of your life again. You need to be the woman I know you are."

"I think you need to get out of my home and leave me alone."

"What?"

"Go away, Rowan. Go back to Phoenix. I don't want you here."

"Willow—"

"You don't know me. We've had sex a few times, but you don't know me. Whatever this was is over."

I stared at her until she turned the TV on and ignored me. I didn't know what happened, but I wasn't the kind of person who was willing to stay where I wasn't wanted. So, I left.

14

WILLOW

The last thing I wanted to do when Rowan walked out the door was sit there and wallow. Sure, it had appeal, but I wasn't going to be that woman. I'd done enough feeling sorry for myself, and I was done with it.

I sent Brittany a text to see if she was available to go out. I needed lots of noise, dancing, and a few drinks so I could forget all about Rowan.

Brittany said she was heading to O'Kelley's to meet up with a new guy but that other people from work would be there, too. I wasn't sure if I wanted to be at O'Kelley's, but it was the best offer I had. Hell, the only offer.

I changed into a pair of skinny jeans and a silky, purple tank top. I grabbed my coat and added gloves and a hat and walked out into the dark night.

O'Kelley's was busy, but Brittany was always easy to spot. She yelled and threw her arm around me when she saw me. "I'm so happy you came!"

"Me, too," I said, hoping I enjoyed myself half as much as she already was. "I need a drink."

"Hell, yeah!" Brittany shouted in my ear. "Someone get this bitch a drink!"

A glass was pressed into my hand. I didn't even care what it was. I turned it up and drained the glass, slamming it down on the table when it was empty.

"Woohoo!" Brittany screamed. "We need to dance!"

Brittany pulled me on the dance floor. I threw my head back and pushed away all thoughts of Rowan and Ramsey and Melody. Someone handed me another drink, and I finished that one, too.

A new song came on, and Brittany declared it was her favorite. She threw her arms in the air and danced in a circle, singing along to every word. I danced with her, letting her energy rub off on me. Going out was a good idea.

As the night went on, I danced with Brittany and the rest of our friends and whatever guy wanted to dance with me. I kept drinking, not worrying about anything other than enjoying my night.

My heart pounded and sweat cooled my body. The alcohol made my head fuzzy. For the first time in way too long, I felt good. I didn't care about my sister or Rowan or anyone else. I was only concerned with myself.

I headed to the bathroom and grinned at the flushed reflection in the mirror. I needed a night out. A night of fun without anyone else to tell me what to do. I didn't need to worry about Melody trying to ruin my relationship with Rowan like she thought I almost ruined hers.

Brittany was at our table when I got back from the bathroom. She was drinking a glass of water and offered me one.

"So you don't have a hangover tomorrow," she explained.

I nodded and chugged the water then poured myself another beer. I was looking to forget, not to be responsible.

Brittany led me back to the dance floor. We danced together as the world got a little fuzzier around the edges. I was feeling good. My body was weightless as I moved. My mind welcomed the release. I didn't think about anything or do anything. I just enjoyed the blissful tingle running through my body thanks to the alcohol.

"I need to rest," Brittany said, dragging me off the dance floor.

I nodded and followed her, falling onto a chair. The chair moved on me and I landed on the floor instead.

"Are you okay?" Brittany asked with a loud laugh. "You totally missed the chair."

I looked up at her and laughed. "I thought it was right there."

Piper came over with another pitcher of water and asked if I was okay.

"I'm great! I'm single and young and ready to have fun," I told her.

"Do you need someone to help you get home?"

I shook my head. "Nope. I'm good."

"Are you sure?"

I nodded and dismissed her with a wave.

"She's such a bitch," Brittany said, glaring at Piper's back.

I opened my mouth to agree but snapped it closed. Piper was always nice to me. She talked to me like I was a person instead of like I was scum. And she cared. Like Rowan did. Like Melody once did.

"She's not a bitch," I told Brittany. "Piper is trying to be nice."

"Whatever. She's friends with your sister. She's probably trying to find out something about you to use it against you. Don't start thinking anyone who knows your sister is nice to you because you're so great."

"Wow, how do you really feel about me?"

Brittany scoffed. "Don't act like I'm your best friend or something. We work together and drink together, but that's it. You'd ditch me in a heartbeat if someone better actually liked you. You're just as big of a bitch as I am, which is why no one likes you, Willow."

I drew back at the venom in her voice. She hated me. She pretended to be my friend, but she didn't like me at all. She was the only person I thought I had left, but I didn't even have her. "You're so—"

"You should climb down off your high horse and shut the hell up, Willow. Because whatever you're about to say about me is something you can say about yourself. You're only here because the boyfriend dumped you and your sister dumped you and everyone you've ever known dumped you. Don't you think, after a while, that maybe it's not all of them who are so shitty. Maybe it's you?"

Her words hit the mark and nearly knocked me out of my seat. I leaned back hard, gaping at her.

Brittany stood. "See you around, Willow." She walked away, leaving me at the table alone. I stared at the empty glasses and the spilled beer and wanted to cry. It pretty much described my life. A waste.

I poured myself another beer and drank it while I watched the people around me move and laugh and talk. Everyone else was enjoying themselves. They were having fun and happy. And then there was me.

I drank another beer and when Piper came over again, I asked her for a shot of vodka.

"How are you getting home, Willow?" she asked softly.

"I'm walking."

"Are you sure you can make it?"

I took a breath and looked up at her. "I know you're being nice, and I appreciate it, but I honestly don't think anyone else would care if I fell on my way home and froze to death."

"That's not true, Willow."

I shrugged. "It kind of feels like it is."

"Laura is still here. Why don't you let her walk you home?"

"Laura is a friend of Melody's."

"She asked if you're okay."

I waved my hand, hoping Piper would bring me the drink and leave me alone. I didn't want to talk to anyone. I didn't want to think about anyone. And I didn't want to need anything from anyone. I learned my lesson. Letting people in meant giving them the power to hurt you. I'd been hurt enough for one lifetime.

Piper brought back the vodka. I smiled at her. She pressed her lips together, but her brows narrowed at me.

I drank the shot and decided it was time for me to go. I had no reason to be there any longer, and I was getting beyond drunk to the point where I would get introspective and weepy. I didn't need witnesses for that.

I walked outside, the cold air slapping me in the face. It threatened to chase away the buzz I had going, but the alcohol was too strong. I took a few steps and leaned against the building for support.

"Can I walk with you?" someone asked from behind me. A woman's voice, which was the only reason I didn't scream.

I turned and saw Laura standing behind me, smiling.

"I live close to you and thought we could walk together. If you don't mind."

"Suit yourself," I told her.

She stepped up next to me and wrapped an arm around my waist. She was sturdy, like she was completely sober. I leaned into her unintentionally, but she didn't falter. She just kept walking like we did this every weekend.

"Who's your friend?" Laura asked.

"She's not my friend."

"Why not?"

"Because she's a bitch. And I'm a bitch. And no one likes a bitch."

"I don't think you're a bitch," Laura said.

I laughed. "Yes, you do. You're friends with my sister, so you know I'm a bitch."

Laura shook her head. "I think you're hurting, and maybe a little scared, and I think it's hard to accept that everyone jumped to conclusions about you, but maybe we were off base doing that."

"Why are you being nice to me?"

"Because your sister is a friend of mine, and Melody doesn't want anything bad to happen to you. She worries about you, even if she's not sure how to say that. And because I'm a nurse and it's in my DNA to help people."

I snorted. "You can't help it. I guess that's as good a reason as any to be nice to me."

Laura shifted my weight so I was standing a little more upright. "I never got to know you before your falling out with Melody, but she really does think the world of you. She misses you. I think she doesn't always know how to say that, but she does."

"How would you know?"

"Because I see people at their lowest. Not all of us can handle it. Fear and sadness show up differently in everyone. And that's on the person feeling it, not the person it's directed to. I'm not saying what you did was okay, but maybe Melody would have been able to forgive you by now if she wasn't so afraid."

I drew in a sharp, cold breath. "I'm afraid she'll never be able to forgive me."

"Which is why you haven't apologized?" Laura guessed.

I nodded.

"And I think if you could apologize, Melody would probably forgive you."

"But you don't know?"

We stopped at my door and Laura shook her head. "No, I don't. But Melody brings you up at girls' night a lot. I think it's because she misses you and wishes you were a part of her life again."

"Well, maybe one day." I unlocked my door and opened it.

"Are you okay alone tonight?"

I nodded. "Thanks for walking me home."

She smiled. "Drink some water and take some ibuprofen. Try to get some sleep, Willow."

"Thanks."

She hesitated then hugged me quickly and walked down my steps and into the night. She turned back toward town and disappeared around the front of house.

I went inside and collapsed on my bed. My head spun, so I put my foot on the ground to stop the spinning. It wasn't long before sleep pulled me under, without water or ibuprofen.

MY HEAD WAS POUNDING when I woke up. I groaned and rolled out of bed, hoping I could take some ibuprofen before my headache got worse.

I downed some water and the meds and headed to the kitchen to find some breakfast. Toast sounded better than anything else, so I popped a few pieces into the toaster and started the coffee.

When everything was done, I sat on the couch with the remote. I flipped to something I didn't have to pay much attention to and ate my breakfast.

I felt better by the time I was done and decided to take a shower. I cleaned up the kitchen and was about to leave the room when there was a knock on my door.

I didn't know who it could be, but no one stumbled to my door, so I opened it without asking who it was.

Big mistake.

It was Melody.

"Are you okay?" she asked. Her eyes scanned my body, evaluating me.

I wrapped my arms around myself and nodded. "I'm fine."

"Laura said you were really drunk last night."

I shrugged. "So?"

"I was worried about you."

"Why? You were pretty clear the other day that I don't matter to you."

"You're my sister, Willow. I'm always going to love you and want the best for you."

I wasn't sure what to say about that. I stared at her.

"Can I come in?" she asked.

I nodded and took a step back to let her in. Melody looked around my apartment like she'd never seen it before. I tried to see it through her eyes. My apartment was nothing compared to her home. It was small with secondhand furniture and mismatched everything. But it was all mine. I loved my sister's house and the way she'd made it a cozy place for her family, but my apartment was all mine.

Melody and I stood looking at each other. I wondered if I should offer her something, but I didn't have much to offer. I didn't have guests. Ever.

"How are things with Rowan?" Melody asked.

I scoffed. "Over."

"Why?"

"Why are you here, Melody?"

"I miss you."

"You...what?"

"When I saw you the other day...I tried to pretend I

haven't been bothered by not having you in my life, but I miss you."

I drew in a breath. "I'm sorry, Melody. I'm so sorry. I never should have...I'm sorry about everything. I never should have kissed Ramsey and I never should have twisted things or—"

"It's not all on you. Things weren't right with Ramsey after Steven. And I turned to you, not him. I didn't know how to talk to him."

"I didn't help anything. I'll never be able to forgive myself for what I did to you guys. I never should have tried to get between the two of you. I...I have no excuse."

"I need to know something," Melody said.

"What?"

"Are you still in love with Ramsey?"

I shook my head. "I don't think I ever was. I said I was, but Ramsey was safe. I couldn't get hurt if I loved him because he was yours. At first, I wanted what you had and convinced myself I could only have it with Ramsey, but once you two got married, he was safe. Boys were never interested in me, and men weren't any better. I was the fat girl, the one who was overlooked. Ramsey saw me, so I latched on to him. But I don't think I ever really loved him. Not the way you did."

Melody was quiet for a minute, letting my words sink in. I hoped she knew I was being honest, and that I really was sorry for what I did.

"What happened with Rowan?"

I shrugged and shook my head. "I messed everything up. I saw him with you at Cracked and..."

"Nothing happened between us," Melody said.

"I know. But everyone tells him to stay away from me. To not get involved or to end things or whatever. I figured you were doing the same thing. I just...I tried not to care when the rest of them did it, but when I thought you were telling him I wasn't worth it, I couldn't handle it."

"I wasn't doing that, Willow. I was asking him if you were doing okay. Ramsey mentioned you two were seeing each other, but I didn't realize how serious it was until he showed up at lunch. I've missed so much of your life. I don't want to miss more."

I inhaled a shaky breath. "I don't want to miss more either, but I know you don't trust me."

Melody shrugged. "I think I trust you more when you're involved with a guy like Rowan. He really likes you. I think you should patch things up with him."

I smiled. "I don't think that's possible. I told him to go back to Phoenix. He's not going to want to see me again."

"Something tells me you're wrong about that. I think you should try. For me."

I rolled my eyes and smiled. Whenever we wanted to convince each other to do something growing up, we would always say it was a favor. I could never deny my sister. Even when I really wanted to hide from Rowan forever.

15

The hard part about finding someone when you didn't know where they lived was you had no idea where to look. Melody didn't have his address, and I wasn't willing to ask James or anyone else. The fewer people who knew about my pending humiliation the better.

Melody wanted to come with me to find him, but she'd already missed enough time with her family for me. And again, I didn't want witnesses.

I went to O'Kelley's first, but he wasn't there. I stopped by Cracked and came up empty again. I wandered around town a little, hoping I might run into him, but by midday, I admitted I needed a plan instead of just to wander.

I grabbed lunch from Just Tacos and sat alone in a booth trying to come up with a good idea. Saturdays meant half the town was at Jones Family Maple Farm when the weather was good, but during the winter, it was quiet. Still, I didn't have any better ideas.

The parking area around the gift shop was quiet, but there were a few cars. And at the end of the line, one motorcycle. My heart jumped and started to pound when I saw it. He was there.

I turned off my car and took a few deep breaths. I stared at myself in the rearview mirror and tried to give myself a pep talk, but I was all out of encouraging words. Melody forgave me, but she was my sister. We had a lifetime of history. Rowan…he didn't owe me anything. I loved him, but I threw him away at the first sign of betrayal. Betrayal that never even happened and wasn't his fault.

I closed my eyes. He deserved better than me. I needed to leave before he saw me because I wasn't good enough for him.

A knock on my window startled me. My eyes snapped open and lifted to the person standing next to me. "Shit."

"Open the door, Willow," Rowan said.

"I was just leaving," I replied.

"Bullshit. Open the door."

I should have just started the car and peeled out, but I couldn't. I needed one last look at him. One last minute near him. Then I would let him go.

I opened the door a crack, barely wide enough that the cold air rushed into my car and started to chill me.

"Get out."

I sighed again and did as he asked. I closed the door behind me and leaned against my car.

"What are you doing here?"

I glanced around and shrugged. "I come here all the time for syrup."

"Bullshit. Again. Why are you here?"

"I was just out for a drive?"

"One more chance," he said sternly.

"Fine," I huffed. "I was looking for you, but I'm leaving now. I shouldn't have come here."

I turned to open the door, but he slapped a hand on it and held it closed. I turned back to him and glared.

"Just let me go, Rowan."

"Why were you looking for me?" he asked.

I drew in a deep breath and stared up at the only man I'd ever really loved. When I was searching town, it was so easy to imagine what I would say to him. To think about all the words that would flow easily from my lips to tell him how sorry I was. But standing in front of him, I was paralyzed. I was terrified.

All my life, I'd lived in the shadows. I didn't date because it was easier not to get attached to anyone. I didn't have close friends for the same reason. The only person who ever mattered to me was Melody. Our parents were...we weren't close to them, but we had each other. And she was the only person I needed, so I didn't bother to try to find anyone else to share my life with.

But that meant I never learned how to apologize to people. I never learned how to tell someone I screwed up. With Melody, I could always say I messed up and I was sorry, and she would forgive me. But anyone else...I never cared enough to try to repair any other relationship. Even saying sorry to Melody this time was harder because it wasn't a little thing that I had to apologize for. It was huge. Just like apologizing to Rowan was huge.

"I'm sorry I was such a bitch to you. I never should have pushed you away or gotten so upset that you had breakfast with Melody. And I shouldn't have told you to go back to Phoenix. It was mean and I was rude and I wanted you to know I'm sorry."

I made another move to leave, but his hand was still on my door, stopping me from going anywhere.

"Why?" he asked.

"Why what?"

"Why are you sorry?"

"Um, what?"

"Are you sorry because you know what you said was wrong or because you think you hurt me or because you think you should apologize or something else?"

"All of it. Sure, I guess. I was mean. I shouldn't have been so mean to you."

"Why?"

"Because I love you, okay? Is that what you wanted me to say? Because I love you. Because I was scared that you were finally going to listen to someone who said to stay away from me because it was my sister. Because of all the people who told you I wasn't worth it, she's the one who knows the best that I'm a pain in the ass and can't be trusted or whatever."

"She never said I should stay away from you."

"Yeah, I know."

His brows went up, and his dark eyes scanned my face. "How do you know?"

"She came to see me this morning. She...I apologized to her for everything."

"Really? Is it apology Saturday and no one told me?"

I rolled my eyes at him and pressed my lips together. It was getting hard for me to keep my emotions in check. I told him I loved him and he barely acknowledged it. Not that I blamed him, but it hurt. I put myself out there, and he was rejecting me.

"Yeah, well, I just wanted you to know I'm sorry. I'll go now. Enjoy the rest of your day."

I turned back to my car, but his hand didn't move.

"You need to remove your hand from the door so I can go," I said softly. The tears were getting closer, choking my throat and making it harder for me to speak.

"No."

"Please, Rowan."

"I haven't accepted your apology yet. Don't you want to know if I forgive you?"

I shook my head. "You don't have to forgive me. I understand if you don't want to. I don't deserve it. I was cruel and heartless and you should have better than that."

"What if I happened to love cruel and heartless?"

I scoffed. "No one loves cruel and heartless."

He leaned closer to me. "I do, Willow."

The meaning of his words filtered through my mushy brain and sank in. Was he? No. But…was he?

My chest rose as hope tried to fill me. I pushed it back out, not willing to believe that much. He knew the horrible things I'd done. He knew who I was. I treated him like shit. There was no way he loved me.

"Look at me, Willow."

I squeezed my eyes shut and took a breath. I let it out slowly and turned to face him, lifting my gaze to his.

He didn't give me time to say anything before he pressed his body against mine and sealed our lips together. He licked his way into my mouth, and groaned when my hands slid up his chest.

His hands wrapped around my waist, pulling me tightly to him. I sank into him, enjoying the feel of him against me. His tongue teased mine as his fingers found their way under my coat to my skin.

When he pulled back, he rested his forehead against mine. His eyes stayed closed. "Don't shut me out, Willow. If this is going to work, you need to trust me. And I need to trust you. I can't handle you not listening to me or thinking you know what happened."

"I know. And I'm sorry. For so many things. I haven't ever had a real relationship. I've had guys I sleep with on occasion, but I've never gotten close to anyone."

"Me neither. I never wanted to get close to anyone. Being

a cop made it hard. I loved the rush of the job and the fast pace. But everything is different here. It's slower and I guess I needed that. But I also needed you."

"You needed me?" I blurted.

He brushed my hair behind my ear and nodded. "I did. I still do. When I got here, I hated the idea of being banished to a place like this. The job was boring. For someone who's only ever had work, I was miserable. But when I met you, life got more interesting. You were the spark I was missing. I loved seeing it in your eyes and feeling it whenever you kissed me. I never thought I'd find that in another person."

"You didn't?"

He shook his head. "No, Willow, I didn't. But you're different. You're special. And you're mine."

I scoffed and pulled away from him. "I don't belong to anyone."

He smirked at me. "That's what I'm talking about right there. I love that. And I love you."

"You do?"

He grinned and kissed my throat. "I do love you. And because I love you, I wasn't ready to give up on us yet. I was pissed at you, but I knew you'd come around. I did not expect Melody to be the one who made you see the light, but I'm happy you two made up. I'm a little surprised you're upright today."

"The cold is helping my headache."

He chuckled. "It sounded like you had quite the night."

"You knew about that?"

He raised an eyebrow. "Do you really think anything is going to happen in MacKellar Cove without the entire town finding out about it?"

"I can think of a few things the entire town doesn't know about. Like that thing you do with your tongue. Or the thing you do with your fingers. Or the thing you do with your cock."

I knew better than to provoke him, but it was far too easy to get a rise out of him.

He leaned against me, trapping me between the door and his body. I looked up at him, daring him.

"You like to fight dirty, don't you?"

I grinned. "That's not the only thing I like to do dirty."

He pressed his body to mine and paused a breath away from my lips. "You might kill me."

I smiled. "It'll be worth it."

"Hell, yes, it will be."

ROWAN FOLLOWED me back to my place and shared a few more things with me that the entire town didn't know. Like how much he loved me and wanted to stay.

I was teaching a yoga class that afternoon and he insisted on joining me for it, even though I told him he didn't have to.

"Do you really think I'm going to miss out on seeing you or having you touch me to make sure I'm in the right position?"

"I'll have to do the same for all the students. You know that, right?"

"As long as they're all female," he growled.

I shook my head. "It doesn't matter. It's my job to make sure people are safe and getting the most benefit out of the class."

"Then I better come to all your classes so none of the men get any ideas."

"Like you do?" I asked him.

He glared at me then stalked across the room toward me. I squealed and ran away, but Rowan chased me until he caught me. He picked me up and started carrying me to the bedroom.

"We need to go!" I argued.

"You can be late."

"No, I can't. I like this job. And if I'm going to keep it, I need to show up on time."

He growled again and set me down. "After class, you're all mine."

"I'm all yours all the time."

He leaned in and kissed my neck. "I like the sound of that."

Class was uneventful until afterward when Sylvia asked to speak to me.

"The students really respond to you," she said.

"Thank you. I'm enjoying teaching."

"Good. You're a natural. I really hope you decide to stick around."

I smiled. "I have. I would love to accept your offer if you're still up for it."

"Really? That's great news. I'm so happy to hear you say that. I love doing this, but I like having other people around. I think we work well together."

"I agree."

"We can talk about all the details later. Right now, I think someone is waiting for you." Sylvia smiled at Rowan. "Hello, Officer."

"Hi, Sylvia. How are you?"

"Very well. Thank you for whatever you did to make her decide to stay."

He blushed and grinned. "You're welcome."

We waited for Sylvia to lock up the studio and all left together. Rowan and I went back to my apartment, where he asked me to demonstrate a few of the yoga poses I used in class.

After another shower, he said, "We need to go out tonight. Celebrate your new job."

"Or we could just stay in."

"Or we could see if Melody and Ramsey want to get together."

I tensed. "It might be too soon for that."

He pulled his phone out of his pocket and showed me the screen. "She's been texting me all day, begging me to let her know everything. She's already invited us over."

I couldn't help but grin. I never thought I'd repair my relationship with my sister, but to also get a great guy? I had to be dreaming.

"We don't have to," I told him.

He shook his head. "Don't start to freak out on me again. All of this is good."

I took a breath and nodded. It was good. Life was good. It had been a while since I'd felt that way, but it was true. Life was good. And it was all thanks to Rowan.

EPILOGUE

LAURA

I sprinkled powdered sugar over the top of the raspberry frosting and grinned. The cake looked perfect. And the crumbs that fell off into my mouth were delicious. My mouth was already watering.

I snapped the cover in place over the top and pulled on my coat. With the cake in hand, I headed over to Book Boyfriends Unlimited for girls' night.

The sky was dark, but a hint of light lingered over the water. Everything was calm and peaceful and perfect. I still couldn't believe I lived here sometimes.

Finley let me into the store and reached for the cake while I took off my coat. "How is it? Did you try it?"

I shook my head. "I ate a few crumbs, and tasted the frosting, but I haven't eaten a piece yet. It smells amazing." The recipe was one she helped me find. The last book we read for book club had a baker as the hero and the things he did with frosting made us all want to run out and find a baker of our own.

"Well, without a sexy man to rub frosting all over me and

lick it off, I don't think it'll compare to the book, but it'll be a close second," Finley said with a grin.

I laughed. "True." I followed her to the back where Blake and Karissa were sitting. I said hi to them and they asked what I made.

"She made the cake from the book," Finley told them. Someone knocked and took her back to the front.

"No, you didn't," Karissa gasped. "Oh, man. Now I'm going to wish I'd accepted one of those dates."

"You had dates and didn't accept?" Blake asked.

Karissa sighed. "I have a really hard time not looking up these guys. And when I do, they're never as good as they seem before I know who they are. One was my dentist."

"Dr. Percy is on Book Boyfriends Wanted?" I asked her with a laugh.

Karissa rolled her eyes. "Yep. And I was matched with him."

"Laura has a new match," Piper said, walking in with Finley. "Are you telling them about him?"

I shook my head as Blake, Finley, and Karissa scoffed.

"You're letting me ramble and you didn't mention you have someone new. Jeez, girl, you're racking up the matches. I'm totally jealous of you," Karissa said.

I laughed. "I'm done waiting around for Mr. Right to show up. I'm enjoying Mr. Right Now and figuring out what I do and don't like in a man."

"Good for you," Blake said.

Another knock on the door took Finley away.

I shrugged. "I spent way too long pining for Nico and he's not interested. It's not worth my time to sit around and hope he sees me one day. I'm moving on and I will find someone else."

"I still think you should have told him," Piper said. "You never know what a man is thinking. He could have been waiting for you to say something. He's your boss, and if he asked you out, you could go after him for harassment."

I shook my head. "Nico is constantly dating someone else. He has a woman in Syracuse that he meets up with every time he goes there, and I'm sure he has other women around here. I'm not going to make a fool of myself and then have to work with him every day. I love my job too much to risk it."

"Yeah, but you love him, too," Finley said.

I shrugged. "Doesn't matter. Hey guys." Melody, Willow, Elise, and Trinity grabbed seats. "Did you all come together?"

They shook their heads. Melody said, "Willow was with me, and Elise and Trinity walked up when Finley was letting us in. Just good timing."

"Even better timing that we can now eat the cake Laura made. It's from the book," Karissa told them.

"No way," Elise groaned. "I might need to take some of this home with me later."

"I'm happy to share the recipe," I said with a wink.

Elise nodded. "I'll take it to Mrs. Carter and see if she wants to help me bake it. I think I'll leave out the details of it, though."

"She might love that story," Melody said with a grin.

"I don't know a woman alive who wouldn't love that story," Willow said. She nudged her sister, and they collapsed into a fit of giggles.

It was good to see them together again. Even though Melody didn't come to girls' night when she and Willow were close, having Willow there definitely brought out Melody's silly side. And it made me miss Peyton. She was the only person I'd ever known who felt like a sister to me.

"Have you heard from Peyton lately?" Finley asked as she helped me hand out cake to everyone.

"I was just thinking about her actually. I need to give her a call. I have some vacation time coming up. I might go visit her for a few days."

"How are they doing?" Blake asked.

I nodded. "Good last we talked. Marriage seems to be a success for them. Finally."

"Marriage. I don't know if I'll ever be ready for marriage," Willow said.

"I'm with you, but Colin is wearing me down," Elise said.

"You're thinking about getting married?" Finley asked her.

Elise shrugged. "He is very persuasive."

The rest of us laughed.

"Well, I think marriage is amazing," Blake said. She met Melody's gaze, who also nodded.

"I agree with Blake," Melody said.

"You two don't count," Finley argued. "Neither of you is normal."

"None of us are normal," Karissa argued. "Normal is a myth. We all do what works for us."

"Which is why you developed an app with about a thousand questions in it," Finley said.

"Yeah, too bad I know how to answer them to make it give me someone I think I want. I wish I could turn off my brain for a little while and get matched with someone who actually fits me," Karissa said.

"It'll happen," I assured her. "There are definitely a lot of great men on there."

"I never would have given Ian a chance if it hadn't been for your app," Blake said.

"It gave Ramsey and me a way to reconnect," Melody said.

"It worked for me, too," Elise said.

"And me," Trinity and Piper agreed.

"Me, too," Willow added.

"Look at all these success stories," I told her. "You should be thrilled with what you created, and trust your own process to find you someone great."

Karissa sighed. "You're right. It's amazing. Maybe I need one of you to fill out the survey for me."

"We can all do it," Finley said. "Give me your phone. We'll do it as a group."

"Now?" Karissa gasped.

Finley grinned. "Right now. We'll find you someone amazing. But you have to trust us."

Karissa shook her head. "I'm not ready for that yet. Maybe someone will turn up. And not be my dentist."

Melody snorted. "I'm not going to be able to keep a straight face next time I see Dr. Percy."

"I know, right?" I laughed with her. "We should not know who is on there."

"I didn't tell you his screen name," Karissa said.

"He probably has something that he thinks is really clever, but isn't," Finley said. "I think he's the master of dad jokes."

"I like dad jokes," Blake said with a pout.

"Which is good, because my brother is a master of dad jokes, too," Finley said.

Blake chuckled and nodded.

"You can tell me his screen name," Willow said. "I closed my account."

"Are you that sure things are going to work out with Rowan?" Melody asked.

Willow nodded. "I am. He's amazing. I can't imagine meeting anyone more perfect for me. We're moving in together. As soon as we find a place."

"Seriously? You didn't tell me that," Melody gasped.

Willow shrugged. "I wasn't sure if you would think it was too fast. We've only been dating for a few months."

"If you're happy, I'm happy," Melody said. She hugged her sister and they both laughed.

"And she won't try to steal your husband again," Elise said.

The rest of us gasped. I stared wide-eyed at Elise. She shrugged.

"Too soon?" she asked.

Willow and Melody exchanged a glance then both started laughing. It wasn't long before the rest of us joined in.

"See," Elise said. "Someone had to say it. We were all thinking it."

"True," Melody agreed. "But I really am happy for you."

"Thanks, Mel. I am, too," Willow said.

They picked up their cake and tapped forks. They both took a bite and groaned.

"Holy shit," Willow breathed. "If I'd have eaten this a year ago, I never would have tried to steal your husband. As long as this cake is in my life, I don't need a man."

"Well, in the book we read..."

THANK **you** for reading Willow and Rowan's story! Willow was a tough character to redeem, but she came around in the end. And Rowan was a fun partner for her. One who wouldn't take her crap but loved spinning her up.

The next book in the series is Laura and Nico's book. Laura moved to MacKellar Cove for the chance to work with Nico, but she never expected to fall so hard for him. She's finally giving up on him ever noticing her and moving on. But Nico might have something to say about that! Start His Curvy Nurse today!

WILLOW AND ROWAN'S story isn't completely over. Subscribers get a free, exclusive bonus epilogue of them moving in together! Only available to subscribers! Sign up now!

WHEN JO GETS the job Eric thought his sister should have gotten, he already doesn't like her. She's always wanted to coach, but she never planned on having an assistant who was hoping to see her fail. Fights on the field lead to fights in the bedroom, but only one of them can get what they really want. Start reading In The Dirt now!

ABOUT THE AUTHOR

USA TODAY Bestselling Author Mary E Thompson spent most of her childhood wishing she had a few less curves. She hid in the pages of books because her favorite characters never cared what size her clothes were. Now, neither does Mary, and she writes stories that celebrate women like her. Real women who have curves, chase dreams, and find love, because we should all be happy, no matter our dress size.

Mary spends her non-writing time with her husband and two kids, watching too much TV, cheering for her home-town football team (Go Bills!), and hiding chocolate from her family.

Visit https://MaryEThompson.com/ to sign up for Mary's newsletter, **Romancing the Curves**. Subscribers get free ebooks and other fun stuff, like exclusive, members only content and giveaways, plus are the first to know about new releases and sales!